# THE
# FORBIDDEN
# ROSE

# THE FORBIDDEN ROSE

**A series by**

# C.H FORTENBERRY

# SIMMS BOOKS PUBLISHING
Publishers Since 2012
Published By Simms Books Publishing
Jonesboro, GA

Library of Congress Cataloging in Publication Data

Carla H. Fortenberry

**The Forbidden Rose**
**ISBN: 0692600981**

Printed in the United States of America
Book Arrangement by Simms Books Publishing
Transcribed by Judy Hattaway
Edited by Mary Hoekstra
Interior layout by Nidia Roman @ RomanArts
Cover by Ana Cruz @ anacruzarts

# DEDICATION

This book is dedicated to my wonderful and supportive parents, Carlton and Judy Hattaway. Your support, help and encouragement have gotten me to where I am now. Thank you so much. I love you both.

And to my friends and family who have helped bring my characters to life, Jett, Vanessa, Skylar, Darrell, Dee, Phillip, Jessica, Murry, Jamie, John, Tegan, Jeremy, Senea, Mia, Antonio, Brad S., Scott, Eric, Libby, Holly, Emily, Evan, Senea, Mary L, Tim J., and Uncle Rudy, may this magical journey we are on never end.

# ACKNOWLEDGEMENTS

Again I owe thanks to many people without whom this series would not have happened. I must begin by thanking God for giving me the vivid dreams that inspired the characters and events found between the covers of my books.

I owe thanks to my parents, Carlton and Judy Hattaway, for their encouragement, and especially to my mom or "pre-editor". She's the only one who can decipher my spelling, etc.

I also want to thank James R. Simms and Simms Books Publishing, my publishing guru, my dream team maker and cheerleader. You have brought me so far so fast!

Mary Hoekstra! My new editor and guardian angel! Thank you for the work that you performed on my book. I know that you can write a good story but an editor can make it Great!

And to Ana Cruz of Ana Cruz Art. You have a gift of going inside my brain, deep into my imagination, and pulling out just what my characters are supposed to look like. I cannot wait to see you bring faces to all my characters.

And to the friends and family who have played a part in my stories, to Murry, Skylar, Dee, Phillip, Darrell, Jamie, Jett, Vanessa, Jessica. B, Emily, Tegan, Jeramy, Mary L.,  Brad S., Lady, Joseph V, Senea, Scott C., Eric M., Libby, Holly, Tim J.,  and anyone else who has been a part of my story. You all know who you are.

And to DGS and ExpressJet, thank you for putting up with me, always going on and on about my stories, and bouncing ideas off of you guys. And to all the authors I have met along my journey, you have inspired me to never give up, even when I feel like I have hit a wall or two. You all know who you are... from the author who guided me to the artist Ana, to the author I met at Comic Con, who wrote about a wonderful elf, and to the Disney author who showed me even villains have kids.

I would like to thank my wonderful husband, Darrell for your patience and putting up with my long hours of typing; my missing family trips because I had to go to a book signing or a convention; and allowing me to follow my dreams and spread my wings.

And this whole story would never have happened without YOU, Skylar. You were the seed to my Murry Rose. And as you grow to be the man I know you can be, so does My Rose grow to the Story I know it will become. Let's enjoy this journey together.

And finally, to all my readers, I am so grateful that you are still reading my story and that you have written wonderful reviews and have given me wonderful ideas for new stories about some of my characters who might have a book of their own. Never stop dreaming. Dreams have no age limit.

And to those students out there who suffer with Dyslexia or any other learning problem, don't think of it as a problem, think of it as a uniqueness.

Without my own uniqueness, I would never have had the imagination I have and this story would not be what it is now. You just need to find your niche and hold on tight to it and it will take you far! Never give up on your dreams, for I have not given up on mine

I hope you love what you are reading. Please tell others and continue this wonderful journey with me.

# *PRELUDE*

My name is Murranda, but many of my friends call me Murry. I was raised by my father, Rudolpho Delarenzo, in a privileged household. I thought I knew all there was to know about my father, my late mother and myself but now I've learned that wasn't so.

Some time ago, I admitted to myself that there was something missing in my life. I didn't know what it was but I knew I had to search for it. So, in spite of my father's protests, I set out on a journey to find that mysterious *something*.

I didn't go alone. My fairy friend, Glitz, has been my constant companion. Along the way I met many more friends, some of whom joined us. You will get to know them as we continue on our adventures.

Before I left my father, I gave him a very special rose. This rose, which I named the "Murry Rose," allowed him to follow my progress and see everything I was doing, everywhere I went, and whether or not I was in trouble. He knew when I met friends and when I met enemies. I also gave a duplicate of the Murry Rose to each of the friends I met along the way, but who were unable to join me on my travels.

The Murry Rose is one of the reasons for the problems I am having now with my father. The other reason for our problems is the secrets he has kept from me.

My travels have led me to the Shadow Land and the Dark Prince. I was warned to stay away from here, but circumstances caused me to do the very thing I was warned against. When my father saw that I had met the Dark Prince, he feared I was in trouble, thus he came, expecting to force me to return home with him. But that was not going to happen. Since I've been here, the Dark Prince has revealed many things about my parents that my father didn't see fit to share with me. Now I intend to stay in the Shadow Land and learn more about my heritage.

There is another reason I must stay. I am still trying to find that illusive *something* I've been looking for, and now I need to learn more about the *Prophesy* no one wants to reveal to me.

# Chapter 1

After Murranda confronted her father and friends about all the secrets they had been keeping from her, she looked toward Prince Demitri and they both quickly vanished from the scene. Murry's friends convinced her father, Rudy, not to worry about her, reminding him that it was the Weekend of Peace in the kingdom. Every year, Xeenoephillia celebrates the reunion of the twin sisters, Phoebe the gypsy, and Pheonna, the dark sorceress. They assured him his daughter would be fine, and he would most likely see her before the lavish Masquerade Ball later that evening.

As part of the weekend celebration, competitive games were held and they all needed to get back to the arena where the competitions were still taking place. The next event was to be a fighting competition between Jezzica and Emily, the Spider Vamp sisters, and Jett the Elf and Phoenix, his friend.

While everyone headed toward the arena, Pheonna, the evil sorceress, returned to her balcony, where she and her sister had been viewing the games. Following her were two, small, black widow spiders. The spiders used their webs, transforming themselves into the Spider Vamp sisters.

Jezz said, "Did you hear that Sorceress? It seems our little Murranda is having many doubts about everyone. She's finding out whom she can and can not trust." As she spoke, she tapped her long fingernails together and there was an evil look in her eyes.

"That may be true," added Pheonna, "but the more doubts she has about everyone else, the closer she is drawn to our prince."

"Well, isn't that a good thing? The closer she gets to our prince, the closer we get to the Prophesy," Emily said with a gleam in her eye.

"That may also be true," said Pheonna, "but I should be the one sitting by his side as queen, not that naive little girl!"

A confused Jezz looked at Pheonna and said, "We thought you wanted her to come to the castle so the Prophesy would come to pass."

"I DID, when I thought Demitri was going to use her like he planned to use her mother, then find a way to get rid of her. Now I can see there is more going on between the two of them than even they realize. I CAN'T have that happening."

Pheonna slammed her staff to the ground and sparks flew. Jezz and Emily exchanged looks of fear and confusion.

"Now I am hoping my next plan of action will solve my problem."

Simultaneously, Jezz and Emily asked, "What is that?"

Pheonna looked at them, gave an evil laugh, and said, "Let's just say that after our dear, sweet Murry attends her first Masquerade Ball you may get to see a whole different side of her. Now, don't

you two have a competition to get to? You don't
want to keep your elf friend Jett and his fiery little
Phoenix waiting, do you?"

Jezz and Emily darted off to the center of
the arena.

As the Spider Sisters rushed to the arena to
battle Jett and Phoenix, Pheonna began working on
her next plan to get rid of poor Murranda. In a blaze
of bluish smoke, she transported herself into the
castle's hallway, until she was right in front of
Murranda's room. She looked around to see if
anyone was in the castle. Seeing no one, she quickly
turned herself into a bluish, smoky mist and slid
through the crack under the door of Murry's room.
She headed to the dresser and closets, and finally,
the nightstand, until she found what she was
searching for.

She took one of Murranda's Murry Rose
seeds. It was wrapped in her handkerchief on the
nightstand. In the thick, bluish mist, the seed floated
out of the room through the crack under the door

and back into the hallway. There, Pheonna formed back into herself.

She held and rolled the seed between her long fingers, musing, "Now let's see how you can help me with my next plan so I can, once and for all, get rid of everyone's precious Murry." As Pheonna was about to leave the castle hallway and return to her balcony where her sister Phoebe was waiting, she heard banging, things being broken, then something screeching. She went to investigate.

When she reached the place where the sound originated, she encountered a band of drunken pirates, trying to steal some of the prince's possessions. One of the pirates was trying, as well, to grab Cozmo the Golden Owl, who was being protected by the prince's servants.

Cozmo was screeching, yelling and clawing at the face of a pirate, who was trying to pluck off his feathers. His feathers were very valuable, because once they were removed, they turned into pure gold.

Cozmo was shrieking, "Get your filthy, grubby, tuna-smelling hands off of me, you drunken lowlife."

"What is going on here?" Pheonna yelled.

"This is none of your concern, pretty little lady. We are pirates and this is what we do."

Pheonna hollered, "Well, I am the prince's sorceress and this is what I do!" She slammed her staff on the ground, causing sparks to fly everywhere, and lifting the pirates into mid-air. They became frozen, except for their heads, so they could still speak and be heard, yelling, "What the…? How the…?"

Then Pheonna walked to one of the pirates, ran her fingers through his dirty, greasy hair, then down his dirty face, trying not to belie her disgust. She asked, "Where, pray tell, is your 'brave' captain? Or are you the captain, my strong, strapping friend?"

The young pirate quickly blushed and started to mumble, "Well, me lady, some of the crew, you see, sometimes thinks of me as their…. "

Then a deep, sultry voice came from behind her, "Arrgh, I be the one you seek, arrgh!" She felt the sharp point of a blade at her mid-back, then felt it moving down her spine to her bum. Pheonna rolled her eyes as she raised her arms and slowly began turning to see their captain.

He was a strapping man, rugged and dirty, with a long, dark beard salted with some gray. He had long, thick, wavy, hair down to his shoulders. His clothes were dingy and torn. He had a hand pistol strapped to his chest and two swords, one in its scabbard and the other in his hand, pointed at Pheonna.

He asked her, "So why ye be looking for me?" He mused, "Unless ye has heard of me reputation with the ladies. If that be the case, may I introduce meself, Captain Darrell Braveheart, at ye service."

"Captain Heartless you mean," said one of the crewmembers, as the others started to laugh.

"Arrg! What was that ye matey," the captain asked.

The pirates quickly looked at each other, saying, "I didn't say anything. Did ye?"

Pheonna approached the rugged captain. She put her finger on the tip of his sharp blade and pushed it through her finger. Magically, the blade began evaporating, from the tip to the handle. The captain's eyes grew wider and wider, yet he tried not to show fear. He could not fathom how to react to what had just happened to his sword.

See his befuddlement, Pheonna asked innocently, "Oh, my Captain, you didn't want that old, rusty sword did you?"

"Well, that sword there be with me through 50 or so battles. I took that there from ye Captain Black Beard himself."

"Impressive," she replied. "But you don't want an old sword like that. It has served its time. I can get you a much better sword, a sword fit for a brave, mighty -- and might I also dare say -- dashing captain of your standards."

He quickly blushed and said, "Ohh! She called me 'dashing'." He cleared his throat and resumed his stern expression.

Pheonna turned toward Cozmo the owl and whispered to him, "You are going to thank me for this later, bird." Then she plucked two of his feathers and quickly transported him to her balcony and her sister Phoebe. She put one feather in her pocket with the Murry Rose seed; the other golden feather she formed into a golden sword, fit for a king.

The captain's mouth watered at the sight of how shiny and golden the sword was. He changed his perspective, saying, "Arrgh, I did not need me rusty, old sword anyway. I be taking that one, if ye don't mind."

"You may have this one, and more like it, if you and your men do me one small favor," Pheonna said, slipping the new golden sword into his scabbard.

She put her arms around the dirty captain, raising his suspicions. He asked, "And what might ye be wanting from me and me crew?"

"Have you heard of a young girl in this castle by the name of Murranda Delarenzo? She is the daughter of Rudolpho and Morinda Delarenzo."

The captain's eyes widened with excitement. "Aye, me lady, I know that family very well. Sir Rudy and the lovely Morinda has sailed me ship many times. Oh, the stories I could tell you, like the one time when…"

Pheonna put her finger over the captain's lip, saying, "As fascinating as your stories may be, Captain, we must save them for another time. As I was saying, their daughter, Murranda, is becoming too close with our Prince Demitri, and I cannot have that. Now this is where you come in, my handsome captain. You are going to kidnap the lady Murranda after the Masquerade Ball has begun. You are to take her on board your fine ship. Then, you will set sail to Dragon's Island, where my gift will be waiting, for you and your fine men, merely for doing me this one favor."

Captain Braveheart asked, "And what shall I do when I get her there?"

Looking at him with such innocence, Pheonna replied, "I don't care what you do with her then. Leave her for the dragons to play with or keep her on your ship to swab the deck. I could care less. Let her be your personal first mate, just as long as she is far away from my prince."

"But how is me crew and I supposed to do this kidnapping with this celebration going on? There will be too many eyes to see us grabbing her."

"Leave all the details to me. Just meet me in my chambers after all the competitions are over. Everyone will be preparing for the Ball. Also, may I say, please feel free to use our bathing room for you and your men to prepare, as well," she said. She waved her hands in front her nose, as if fanning away their stench.

Pheonna added, "Meet me in my chambers and I will give you all the details."

At that, Pheonna let loose her most evil laugh as she dripped the dangling crewmen back to the ground, and vanished in a cloud of bluish smoke.

Despite being quite stunned, the crew and the captain gathered around to look at the captain's golden sword. They all began laughing with excitement, imagining and speculating what gifts were in store for them, after kidnapping Murry and taking her to Dragon's Island.

# Chapter 2

While the other guests in the arena were watching the competitions, Pheonna, the dark sorceress, had been collaborating with Captain Braveheart and his pirate crew. Jett the Elf ran into the arena and came up behind his friend, Phoenix. This startled her so much that she grabbed Jett's arm from behind and easily flipped him over her shoulder. The moment she realized it was Jett, Phoenix halted before she slammed him to the ground. She quickly brought him to his feet, as if by instinct.

Phoenix couldn't believe she had done that to Jett. She didn't know how to react, so she just punched him in the shoulder for scaring her so. Jett couldn't believe what had happened either, but he shrugged it off as she had, and they laughed and hugged each other.

"So, are you ready to battle the Web Weaving Sisters?" Phoenix questioned, with a cute giggly smirk.

"Those two don't scare me. We can take them on," replied Jett. He rolled his eyes and laughed at her question. The two of them walked to the arena holding hands.

"I'm sure you're not scared. In fact, I think you like all this attention."

"Attention? What are you talking about?" Jett gave her a puzzled look.

"What? Are you telling me that you don't see how the Vamp sisters look at you? How they act around you? They are both so taken by you that it is causing a rift between them. It seems that the oldest one won't take NO for an answer."

Jezz insisted, "Well, I have no interest in either of them, so I don't care what she can or cannot take. Neither of them will get me, or have me, or do anything with me."

Jett began walking backwards toward the arena still holding hands with Phoenix. Suddenly, he bumped into the Spider Vamp sisters.

They stood with their arms crossed, looking at him up and down, and so seductively.

"What? You don't want to play with us? I don't understand why not. Do you sister dear?" Jezz asked as they both laughed.

"Let's just get this over with," said Jett. He grabbed Phoenix's wrist and pulled her to the center of the arena. He said to Phoenix, "The faster we beat these two pests, the faster you and I can have some time to ourselves. Just the two of us."

Phoenix laughed, but Jezzica and Emily did not find it a bit funny. In fact, Emily flicked her fingers and shot a thin string of web at Phoenix's feet and made her trip and fall.

"Good one, little sis. I did not know you had it in you," Jezz whispered to her sister.

"Well, I did learn from the best," Emily said, winking at her sister.

Jett spun around to go after the sisters, Phoenix stopped him, saying, "Don't, Jett. Save it for the competition. Just help me get out of this sticky web. Don't let them get to you."

So Jett helped untangle her feet from the web and helped her to stand up. Phoenix kissed him, as the two sisters watched. She knew they would react, and that is exactly what they did.

Jezz and Emily stared at her with evil looks. Emily was about to do something else, but her sister stopped her with, "She's right, sis. Let's save it for the game. I'll have my chance with him. I mean WE'LL have our chance with him yet."

With that, they all moved to the center of the arena to start the competition.

As Jett, Phoenix, Jezz, and Emily neared their places in the arena, Phoebe, the gypsy, saw that Cozmo, the golden owl, appeared out of nowhere. He was still in his cage, but he looked at her and said, "What are you looking at? Haven't you ever seen an owl before? You know you have; you are the one that made me like this, you witch."

Phoebe cajoled him, "Now, now, Cozmo. I'm a gypsy, not a witch. And you know why I turned you into the creature you are now. Unfortunately, I see you still have not learned your lesson. Since you are still full of feathers, I know you have not learned to be selfless."

Phoebe looked intently at Cozmo and told him, "Also, I can tell you have been around other greedy beings. Some of your feathers are missing, and you did not pluck them yourself."

With a smirk, she began preening him to look more presentable for the competition. With just a snap of her fingers, feathers immediately appeared in the areas made bald by greedy plucking. As she worked, Phoebe said "What I am wondering is, who conjured you to pop up here? It must have been my sister But where is…."

Before she could utter the name, "POOF!" Pheonna appeared and asked, "Were you looking for me, sister dear? Sorry, I was handling a matter in the castle that needed my attention. She changed the subject so her sister would not ask what she had been up to and asked, "So who's up next?"

Phoebe gave her sister a suspicious look and wondered what she had been doing, but she shrugged it off and continued to welcome everyone back from their break. Then she began to review the rules of the next competition.

Phoebe explained, "Now this next competition will be Jett from Elfinnea and his friend Phoenix from an unknown region, versus the Spider Vamp Sisters, Jezzica and Emily, from here in the Dark Castle.

When Phoenix's name was mentioned, two dragons looked up from the ground to see this Phoenix person they had heard about. They were talking among themselves when Phoenix spotted them and had the feeling she should know them.

One of dragons had markings similar to ones Phoenix had on her own skin. Those were markings of flames on her arms and legs. She had always ignored them, because they were just a part of her.

When she saw the same markings on the

face and body of one of the dragons though, she couldn't help wondering who they were. She shook her head and put those thoughts aside. She needed to focus entirely on what was going on in the arena, and listen to Phoebe explain the rules of the game.

"In this next competition, there will be two teams battling each other. We will look for how well strategy is used in trapping their opponents. We also want to see how fast they can get out of a trap or how well they can block opponents to keep from getting trapped. We want to see their fighting skills. When we blow the horn, they will stop and retreat back to their respective corners, until the horn sounds again, at which time they will continue. Once both opponents are trapped, or a team retreats and gives up, we will announce the winner."

Then Pheonna shouted, "Are the teams ready?"

They all nodded.

"If my Spider Vamps use their ability to shrink themselves to the size of a small spider, the opposing team will be awarded double points, and if my girls continue shrinking themselves it may result in an automatic loss for the Spider sisters."

"That's not fair!" Yelled Emily. "We can't help if we…"

Jezz put her hands on her sister's shoulders to calm her, saying, "It's okay sis. We've got this competition. We have many more clever tricks up our webbed sleeves. Transforming ourselves into our spider forms is not our only advantage. That Golden Owl is OURS!" She glared right at Cozmo. All Cozmo could do was give a big gulp in fear and try to hide behind Phoebe.

Then the Spider Sisters laughed and with their fingers together formed a shiny, glittery web-like owl that looked just like Cozmo. In the next instant they drew back their web and it retreated into their long fingers. Then both of them formed two hearts out of web and this time blew it over to where Jett was standing next to Phoenix. Jett grabbed the webbed hearts and tore them apart.

The teams faced each other, then turned to face Phoebe and Pheonna, and finally they faced where the Dark Prince should have been sitting, but he was not there. He was still somewhere with Murry. Everyone wondered where they were.

Then the teams faced the King and Queen of the mainland, and then turned back to each other. The whistle blew and the competition began.

Jezz raised her hands in front of her. Webs shot out of her outstretched fingertips and flew towards Phoenix. The webs quickly encircled her legs and dragged her upwards so she was hanging upside down in front of them, as if the web were made of some indestructible material.

Then, just as quickly as Jezz had immobilized Phoenix, Jett came in, cut the web down with his elf blade, and freed Phoenix. As he cut it however, the web began sticking fast to his blade. That gave him a fantastic idea. He ran as fast as he could, around and around Jezz, each circuit tying her tightly with her own web.

With a seductive leer, Jezz asked Jett, "How did you know I liked being tied up?"

The crowd cheered at the sound of the official horn. Pheonna stood and announced, "Point for Jett and Phoenix!"

Emily looked at the sorceress and said, "WAIT! My sister tied Phoenix upside down. Doesn't that at least deserve a point or two?"

"Maybe so, but as soon as she got the girl the elf quickly released her and tied up your sister. And she is still tied up."

"Now, now, sister dear," Phoebe interrupted. "Emily is right. They deserve a point. It was impressive how she grabbed Phoenix so quickly and had her upside down with only her web."

While Phoebe was swaggering about the Spider sisters, Jezz broke free and said, "Oh, you think that was impressive? You haven't seen anything yet."

With a slight wave of her fingers and a knowing laugh, she crafted a huge, web-like net. She swung it around and around her head, then hurled it towards Jett and Phoenix. Phoenix jumped away from it, just in time. She hoped Jett would do likewise, but as Jett was about to jump away, the web fell over him, trapping him in its horrid, sticky threads.

The horn blew again and Pheonna yelled, "Point to the sisters."

Phoenix, with one of her long nails, sliced the net and freed Jett.

During the competition, Phoenix noticed a woman in the crowd and she was marked in the same way as herself and the dragons, except her markings were darker. The woman turned her head to and fro every time Phoenix drew close to Jezz and Emily. When the woman tossed her hair, fiery sparks flew out. The strange woman stared at Phoenix, as if to say, "Do this!"

Phoenix had the disconcerting feeling she knew the strange woman, but didn't know how that could be possible. Phoenix was an orphan and had been raised by gypsies. No one knew much about her past and neither did she. She only knew she constantly changed. New markings appeared; she seemed to be aging too quickly. That thought in mind, when Emily made a spear out of her web and flung it toward her, Phoenix decided to do what the strange woman signaled her to do. She whipped her long hair towards the oncoming, webbed spear. When she did so, her hair suddenly grew longer and longer, seeming to turn into flames, as though it was a fiery torch.

When her hair barely touched it, the webbed spear suddenly burst into flames. The flames grew so long and so fast, they licked at Emily's arm and scorched her. Emily jumped back to stand near Jezz; both sisters were more than shocked at what happened.

Emily sputtered, "How did you…? What did you…?"

Jezz only managed, "Who or what are you?"

Jett ran to Phoenix who was clearly as shocked as everyone else. Jett asked, "Are you alright? How did you do that just now?"

Phoenix was dumbstruck and admitted, "That's just it, Jett, I don't know." She scanned the crowd only to find the strange woman, who was smiling with pride.

The competition continued with kicks and punches, body-slams, blocking, and the hurling of bodies this way and that. As it continued, Jett's sister, Nessa, stood near a watering hole, where horses and other animals came to drink. She cheered loudly for her brother and Phoenix.

Nessa was also practicing how to control the elements, a gift Evanwood, her oldest brother, informed her she had within her. She raised her hands in front of the watering hole and as she did, water from the hole rose and formed a wall. Nessa tried moving the water forward, but if only fell back into the hole. Undeterred, she tried, again and again but to no avail. Nessa became more and more frustrated each time the wall of water fell.

Behind Nessa, a native girl watched and giggled at the funny water. Try as she might, Nessa could not ignore the girl. Between the girl's giggles and her own inability to master her skills, Nessa began doubting herself.

She wondered why she had been given this gift if she couldn't muster up the ability to fully use it. What happened next between Nessa and the giggling native, made her realize that this could be the person her beloved brother Evanwood told her to look for. But then again, she could have sworn he said the one to look for was a male. He had told her the native would have the elements of Earth, Fire, Wind and Water pictured on his arm He would be the one to guide her and teach her how to use her newfound gift.

Meanwhile, as the competition continued, the Spider Sisters continued flirting with Jett, fighting him and Phoenix at the same time. Jezz was obviously getting tired of all this competition and wanted to end it so she could try to get Jett alone. She decided to take matters into her own hands.

Jezz ran to Jett and Phoenix and stood in front of them so closely they could feel her cold breath on their faces. She thrust her arms upward, her long fingers pointing toward the two of them. She crisscrossed her arms and hands, back and forth and back and forth, shooting her web at them. She quickly trapped both Jett and Phoenix in an unbreakable cocoon from their feet to their necks.

Then Jezz walked to Jett and started running her fingers through his dark hair. She looked directly at Phoenix, and in vengeance gave Jett a long, passionate kiss. Jezz knew that would anger Phoenix. What Jezz didn't count on, or expect, was what Phoenix did next.

Phoenix was so furious about what was happening, her face and skin started turning red. Inside the cocoon, something glowed and grew brighter and brighter, until a Ball of fire burst, engulfing both Phoenix and Jett and blowing Jezz out of the way. The cocoon trapping Jett and Phoenix turned into a pile of ashes.

What shocked everyone in the arena, except the strange woman in the crowd, was what happened next to Phoenix.

Everyone could see Phoenix turning into what appeared to be a phoenix dragon. Her wingspan seemed as long as the arena itself. Then Phoenix started to fly around the arena. She flew high in the air.

Nessa kept trying to make the water from the watering hole rise up and move, in order to save her brother from the flames. All she was able to do was bring it up like a wall, then it would fall back down.

The giggling native girl who had been standing behind her came to Nessa and said, "Here, let me help."

The girl held her own hands up and the water quickly formed a wall. Then she motioned the water to go where Jett was, and the wall of water quickly floated over the crowd and landed on Jett. The remaining flames around him were doused.

Nessa was quite impressed by the native girl, but instead of talking to her like her beloved brother Evanwood wanted her to do, she rushed to her brother's aid.

Phoenix, now a huge phoenix dragon, flapped her feathery, fiery wings, creating a massive wind storm that terrified everyone, especially the Spider Vamps. They immediately shrunk themselves into their spider sizes and skittered under the balcony, below where Pheonna and Phoebe were sitting. Then Phoenix looked down at Jett and his sister. Jett was brushing the ashes and web off his body; both he and his sister had frightened and confused looks on their faces. Everyone in the arena shared that same look.

Then Phoenix looked up and saw the two dragons plus another phoenix dragon. It was darker than she, and flew high above the frightened crowd. She heard the horn blow and Phoebe announced, "Since the Spider Vamps broke the rules by shrinking themselves and fleeing the arena, the win goes to Jett and Phoenix."

What should have been an out-pouring of applause was nothing but silence. Phoenix felt all eyes on her. She didn't know what to do. Then the darker phoenix dragon flew down and motioned her to follow. Phoenix looked back at Jett and saw his expression of confusion and fear. So, with tears in her eyes, Phoenix followed the other dragons as they flew away from the arena.

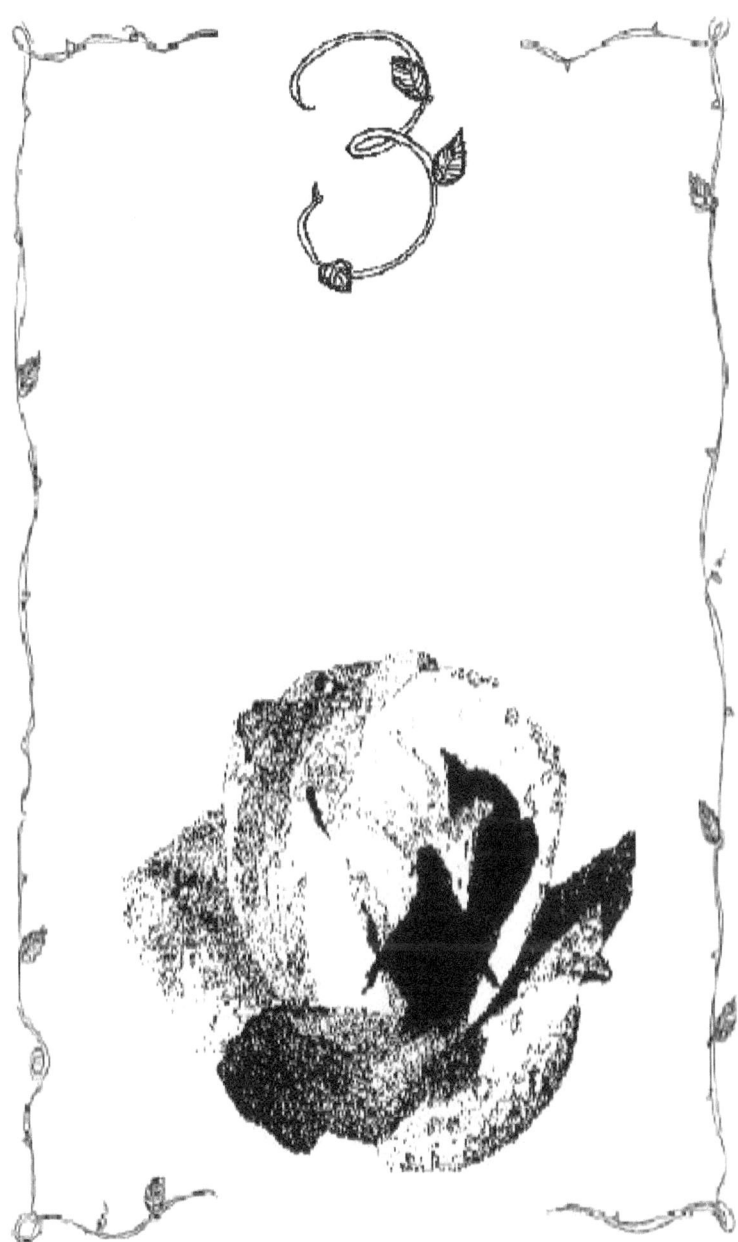

# Chapter 3

Everyone in the arena buzzed about what had just happened. My father and my friends wondered where Prince Demetri and I had gone. I just had to get away because I was having trouble taking in everything I had just learned.

My father had kept secret the fact that he and my mother knew the prince. Through all the stories he had told me as a child, he never once mentioned how they, too, had been in the Shadow Land. Not only was my father keeping secrets from me, but it also seemed my so-called new friends were doing the same – as if somehow I was part of some kind of Prophesy. I simply needed to leave the arena and all the drama I had heard. The prince could see how distraught I was becoming, so he quickly wrapped me in his cape and we vanished into thin air.

I felt I was in a dream. We were shielded in a fog, moving quickly around the castle property. We reached a ghostly river with a waterfall across from where we landed. We saw what looked like a male and female deer yet they were in a ghost-like form. We could see right through them. They were drinking from the river near the waterfall.

We were standing by a ghostly tree, and I could barely catch my breath. It all happened so fast my knees became weak. The prince caught me before I fell to the ground.

He asked, "Are you okay." I could feel his cold arms around me.

"I'm alright, I was just a little weak in the knees, that's all."

"I guess I can have that effect on people sometimes," he joked, as we both laughed.

I looked around and asked, "Where are we?"

"We are at one of your mother's favorite spots in the kingdom."

"I still can't believe she and my father were here in the past, but he never said anything about it to me." I, Murranda, grew angry again, just thinking about it.

"My dear Murry, I'm sure your father had his reasons for not telling you. He loves you and wants to protect you," the prince said with a tender voice.

He brushed my hair back behind my ear. The feel of his ice cold fingers brushing against my ear gave me goose bumps.

"But protect me from what? This Prophesy everyone keeps talking about?"

"Yes, the Prophesy and also from me and my kind," he said, as he turned his head away from me.

"But you are the ONLY one who has told me anything about my family."

I gently put my hand on the side of his cold face and pulled it back towards me. As he turned my way and looked at me with those piercing eyes, I could feel my heart racing. I didn't understand this feeling I was having for someone I hardly knew. But I do know he is the Dark Prince of the Shadow

Land, and he is a blood-sucking vampire prince. Somehow I have trouble seeing that. He has been nothing but kind to me.

Was the prince kind to me only because this was the Weekend of Peace? Now that I thought about it, the ruby stone in my necklace glowed and vibrated when I was alone with the prince. The necklace was given to me by Phoebe, the gypsy, when I began my journey. It was supposed to warn me when danger was near, but at the time I could not see the danger.

The prince convinced me to replace the stone with a look-alike and keep the real stone in my purse. By doing that, my friends would not be able to see the glow and make me leave the castle, just when I was learning the truths about my mother and family.

Even though my heart was racing, as I stood here in this field so close to the Dark Prince, I could tell the real stone in my purse was not vibrating or glowing, so everything appeared fine.

I looked around the ghostly area and up at the trees covered in spider webs. I said, "This place is spooky, yet at the same time, it is breathtaking."

The prince just laughed.

"What's so funny?"

"Your mother said those exact words when she first came here."

"Well it's true. Those deer over there, for example," I said pointing at the ghostly deer drinking next to the waterfall, "are they spirits, or ghosts, or merely very, very white deer?"

Before he could answer my question I pointed toward the falls. I could see something in the falls with piercing, bright green eyes. It was looking at me through the tumbling water. It looked as though there was a cave behind the water.

"Demitri, it seems we're not alone. Someone is staring at us."

He looked where I was pointing and said, "Oh that is the cave of the Dark Elves. It is the entrance to their kingdom."

"Did you just say Dark Elves? They took Cozmo and struck me with one of their arrows. Thanks to Jett, Nessa, and Evanwood, I was saved."

The look on the prince's face betrayed shock and concern, as did his words, "So you did not die from the poison that is normally on their arrows?"

"Die? No, I'm standing right here in front of you. So I did not die," I responded sarcastically. "What are you talking about?"

Demitri ran his cold fingers again through my hair and behind my ear where he had tucked it before. He then noticed behind my right ear, in the inner part of my hair were a few strands of shimmering white hair. He looked around my head to see if he could see anymore. He didn't find anymore, so he looked down and shook his head. He knew what those strands of white glimmering hair meant. When he noticed that those strands where the only ones in my hair he seemed to breathe a sigh of relief.

I did not understand what was going on. "Is everything okay? You are behaving strangely."

"My Dear Murry," he said with sadness in his voice. "I hate to tell you this, but in fact, you did die."

"What are you talking about Demitri? I didn't! I'm standing right here."

"After you were hit with the arrow, did you feel as though you were someplace else? When you awoke at the elves' village, did the elves say anything about how long you'd been unconscious, or how much blood you lost?"

I thought back to that very moment. I remembered dreaming I saw someone in what looked like a flowing light, or bubble of some sort. Also, I did remember the elves telling me I had lost a lot of blood. They told me, as well, that elf tears could heal someone on the brink of death. Certainly that had to mean I wasn't dead, dead.

"So, are you saying I died and came back to life?" Hesitantly, I asked, "Am I a vampire?" I really did not want to hear the answer.

The prince looked at me and laughed, "Are you craving blood?"

I looked back at him with disgust and said, "No! Ugh, how horrible!"

"Then, no, you are not a vampire."

"How do you know I died anyway? Do you smell death on me?"

"No, you smell quiet lovely."

"You mean 'Yumm' don't you? I know how you vampires are."

"I know by this." He pulled the white shimmering streak of hair away from my ear and brought it up towards my eyes so I could see it.

I immediately grabbed the streak of hair from his cold hands and looked at it closely as I turned away from him. I could not believe what I was seeing.

I became crazed and demanded, "How did I get this? Where did it come from? What's going on? What's happening to me?

First you tell me, if I want to learn something badly enough, all I have to do is want it. Then, POOF! Now I can talk with my hands.

Then you tell me I died once and you show me how my hair is turning white. I need to get out of here. I can't take anymore of this right now. I just want to go back to my room and rest for the Ball tonight."

As soon as those words were out of my mouth, POOF! I was no longer at the prince's sight but, magically, I was in my room in the castle. I looked in the mirror and saw a shining star on my forehead. It frightened me so much that I fainted.

Prince Demitri thought about following Murranda because he knew what was happening, but he deduced that if her father, or anyone else who had been given the 'Murry Rose,' would see what was taking place, they would know she had suddenly returned to her room in the castle. He was sure they would be running to her aid.

So knowing that, he decided to go back to the arena and observe the remaining competitions. He would announce the winners and remind everyone about the lavish Masquerade Ball later in the evening.

# Chapter 4

At the arena everyone was still talking about what happened after the last competition, about Phoenix suddenly, somehow, changed from a young woman to a huge, phoenix-like dragon. People could not believe what they had seen.

Jett didn't know how to react to it all. On the one hand, he knew it was still his beloved Phoenix; on the other hand, he wondered if she was still the same Phoenix, now that she had turned into a massive, feathered, fiery dragon. Would she ever turn back to her human form?

"I need to go after her," Jett said to his sister Nessa, as he dusted off the ashes.

"Jett, don't!" Nessa begged, grabbing at his arm to stop him. "We don't know if she is going to be the same after this. We really didn't know her very well in the first place."

Jett jerked his arm way and exclaimed, "I DO! I know her! "She is still in there somewhere. I have to believe that. She needs my help." With that, Jett departed to find Phoenix.

Nessa was about to follow her brother, when she suddenly felt someone grab her shoulder, and heard a young voice say, "Your brother needs to do this on his own. He'll be all right. There is a different path you must follow now."

Nessa turned around and saw a young native girl with dark skin, and dark, straight hair with downed feathers woven in two thin braids in front of her face. She had dark brown eyes that seemed to have sparkles of gold in them. She had markings all over her body, some tribal, some animal, and some of the five elements.

The clothes she wore looked like they were made of different animal skins, maybe deer and leopard. She had moccasins on her feet. She also wore a unique pendent around her neck. The outside of the pendent was gold and diamond-shaped. The center of it was an ocean-blue stone. Nessa realized this was the same young girl who helped her brother when he was engulfed in flames. She commanded the water from the watering hole to rise up and move to Jett to put out the flames.

"It's YOU! You are the one who saved my brother during the competition. I can't thank you enough. You must be the one my oldest brother Evanwood told me about. You have the same gift as me and can control the elements. Although I'm sure I was told to look for a native man who would teach me to harness my gifts."

"Yes, that was my father," the girl replied. "He knew your brother very well. I'm sorry for your loss. The news of his passing traveled far to my village.

"You see, when my father died, his gift passed on to me. My name is Serena of the Windicca tribe. We live high in the Snowpeak Mountains just outside of your Mainland.

"Most of my people can control the winds, but only very few can control all five of the elements. I was told that once I came into my powers I should look for you and train you in the use of your unique gift."

"Well, if you truly believe my brother Jett will be alright... I just lost one brother and I'm not ready to lose another," Nessa explained. She and Serena walked away as she shared more about their abilities.

At the same time, Murranda's father, Rudy, was walking around the grounds, holding tight to the "Murry Rose." Murranda gave him the rose as a way for him to see that she was safe while on her journey, but to her father, if Murry was anywhere with that vampire prince she was not safe.

Jeffery, Rudy's butler and closest friend; Deena, the unicorn; Glitz and Flutter the fairies; and Gray Sky, the Camilla cat, were also walking with Rudy.

Rudy looked deeply into the white rose. He could see that Murry was still with the prince, somewhere in a wooded field. He noticed a waterfall in the shadow of the rose. He could tell something was going on between Murry and the prince. Then, all of a sudden, Murry simply vanished. For a second, the rose was all white. Before Rudy could panic, the rose started forming shadows again. He saw that Murry was finally away from the prince and it looked as if she was in a bedroom. He could see the light shadowy image of a bed and a dresser.

"Look Rudy!" Glitz said, as he stood on Rudy's shoulder and pointed to the rose. "Murry is okay. She is back in her room in the castle."

"Yes, Glitz I see that." Then he gently grabbed Glitz and Flutter and placed them in Jeffery's hands.

Rudy said, "I must go to her. She needs me. I feel something has happened. I know she must be shaken up about everything that is going on. Let me go to her and we will find you all soon."

"If you get on my back I can take you there much faster," said Sky as he grew into a giant tiger. Rudy could not believe what he was seeing, but he knew Sky was right. He quickly hopped on his Sky's back, handing the rose to Jeffery to protect.

The two of them raced to the castle and Murry's room, hoping to find she was alright.

From the arena, Phoebe, the gypsy, could see what was transpiring with Rudy and the others. She also had one of Murry's roses and was keeping a close eye on her. She saw what had taken place between Murry and the prince. She had seen that Murry had fainted, but then suddenly appeared in her bedroom. When she saw Rudy and Sky head toward the castle, she knew she had to help. With her own magic abilities she vanished from the balcony of the arena to meet them in the hallway of the castle.

Sky and Rudy arrived right outside Murry's door. Sky began shrinking to a smaller size to make it easier for Rudy to climb off.

"Thank you for getting me here so fast," Rudy said as he petted Sky on the forehead. "I still can't believe I rode on a cat. That's something to add to my journal."

Rudy walked to door and started knocking. Unfortunately, Murry was prone on the floor. Rudy knocked louder and louder, frantically calling out, "Murranda it's me, your father. Please let me in Sunshine!"

He tried opening the door himself but with no luck. It was locked. He muttered, "Errrg It's locked," then called out again, "Murranda, honey, please let me in."

Nothing happened.

Just then, a cloud of purple smoke appeared between Rudy and Sky, and in the smoke was Phoebe.

She said, "So, old friend, I see you can't get in. I thought you might be here. I too have one of her roses and saw what was going on, so I came as fast as I could to help. I know an easier way to get in."

She closed her eyes tightly and, by magic, the three of them turned into purple smoke and blew into the room through the crack under the door. Once they were in the room, they returned to their normal forms and saw that Murry was motionless on the floor near the vanity table.

They ran to her and both Phoebe and Rudy grabbed her hands. They began rubbing and patting her hands and face in an effort to wake her. Sky also helped by licking her face and nose.

"Honey, are you okay? Oh, please wake up," Rudy pleaded, with tears in his eyes. "If that no-good prince did anything to hurt my little girl I will..."

I could barely hear what was happening. I started to feel something wet on my nose and cheek as Sky kept licking me. I then heard Phoebe say, "Look, Rudy! She is waking up."

As soon as I opened my eyes to see what had happened, my father held me tight against his chest, telling me, "Oh, Sunshine, you're okay. You had us all scared to death. Did that blood-sucking prince do anything to you?"

"No Father, he didn't. I'm fine. I just fainted, that's all. I passed out because when I was in the ghostly forest, talking to Demitri about my mother -- after all, he is the only one who has truly told me anything about her -- he told me that somehow I once died and then came back to life. He knew this because of this strand of glittery, white hair I have."

I took the piece of glittery hair from behind my ear to show them, then continued, "When I could not take it anymore, I yelled that I really wanted to go back to my room to rest before the Ball later tonight. Before I knew it - PRESTO - I magically ended up here. I was so astonished I fainted."

When I sat up and held out the stand of glittery, white hair, I could tell they knew something about what was going on with me. I could see it in their faces. I noticed a tear in each of their eyes. The only one with no clue of what was happening was Sky.

"Okay," I said in a demanding tone. "I can tell you two know something that you're not telling me. I'm sick and tired of all these secrets. What is going on? What is happening to me? I DEMAND to know EVERYTHING."

Phoebe and my father looked at each other. They knew the secret was about to come out and they needed to tell me everything, even though they really didn't want to. Then they both looked at me.

My father looked into my eyes, took a deep breath, and letting out a sigh he said, "You truly have your mother's eyes, and you look more like her every day." Continuing with some hesitation in his voice, "I prayed her looks, and maybe some of her personality, would be all that you had of her," but you are becoming more and more your mother's daughter. You do have her eyes, her smile, her wonderful laugh and even her strong will and stubbornness, but unfortunately, you have her curse, as well."

"Now Rudy, my old friend, it is not a curse," Phoebe interrupted. "It's who and what she was. You knew this when you met Morinda."

"Well she wouldn't have called it that but I do. With everything that has happened to my family, and everything we have lost, I call it a curse."

I said, looking at both of them with suspicion, "What are you talking about? A curse?" Sky sat next to me and he looked up at me, then at my father and Phoebe, then back at me. He shrugged his shoulders as if to say, 'I don't know.'

"Why did Phoebe just say, 'who and what my mother was'? Why does Demitri think I died and came back? What is this prophesy everyone keeps talking about? How am I a part of it?"

I held my father's hands and looked straight into his eyes, beseeching him, "Father, please, no more secrets. I still can't believe that we had secrets in the first place. It breaks my heart that you have kept all this from me."

"Ever since I can remember, you've taught me to always be truthful and honest, that honesty is the key to any relationship," I told him.

"So how is it that the father who talks about honesty and trust is the very person who has been lying and keeping secrets from me, your own daughter? Yet, you expect me to continue to trust you and look up to you?" I could tell those words really hurt him, but I could not help how I felt.

"You're right, Sunshine, I haven't been completely honest with you. For that I am truly sorry, but I am not sorry for the reason why. Everything I do is to protect you."

"Protect me from what?" I cried out.

I stood up and quickly walked to my vanity mirror to see if the star was still shining on my forehead. It was gone but I rubbed my forehead to see if I could feel something there. I felt nothing.

I said to my father, "You want to protect me from some Prophesy you continue referring to. What's going on Father? What's going on here? No more secrets! One of you must tell me."

Looking up at me, Sky said, "I promise you, Murry, I don't know what's happening. I just wish you would not get involved with that Dark Prince. I don't trust him."

"That may be so, Sky," I replied as I continued rubbing my forehead and wondering what happened to the star that had been there.

I continued replying to Sky, "It seems he is the ONLY one who has been telling me things my family should have been telling me all along."

"I wouldn't believe half the things that blood sucker had to say," Father said, rolling his eyes and whispering under his breath. He quickly stood to help Phoebe to her feet. They walked toward, curious to see what I was looking at in the mirror.

Phoebe noticed how I kept peering in the mirror, checking my forehead. She realized what must have happened to startle me so, and cause me to blackout.

She put her hands on my shoulders and said, "Murry, my dear, you should not be so obstinate toward your father. He means well."

She turned me around to face her and Father and said in a caring voice, "But you are right. It is time that you knew the truth about your family secrets, the good and the bad. Bear in mind, though, my dear, once you know the truth about your family, your life as you know it will never be the same. Knowing the truth may put you in even more danger. Considering what you've heard, are you sure you're ready to know everything about your family's secrets?"

I Looked at Phoebe and then at my father. I could see the concern and fear in their eyes. I took a deep breath and sighed as I walked to stand between them. I put my hands on their shoulders and said, "Yes, I want to know. No, I NEED to know the truth. Now!"

Father and Phoebe looked at each other. They each let out a huge sigh, then Father clasped my hands and led me to the side of my bed.

"Sunshine I think you should sit down. Get comfortable and I will tell you everything."

The three of us arranged ourselves on the side of my bed. I scooted to the middle and crossed my legs so Sky could sit in my lap and I could pet and hug him for comfort. Father and Phoebe sat on either side of me.

I could easily see how heavy this secret was for Father to tell. He fidgeted and rubbed his legs. He found it difficult to even look at me.

"Sunshine, you recall all those pictures of your mother we have around the house, and the locket you have with your mother's picture," he began, reaching to touch the locket I wore around my neck. It was behind the necklace Phoebe had given me.

Father continued, "Have you noticed both you and your mother share the same birthmark, a star on your upper lip?"

"Yes, Father, of course. What about it?" I asked as I covered the birthmark with my hand.

"Do you remember telling Jeffery and me some of the wild and strange dreams you had? You dreamed you left your body and traveled up to the sky, past all the clouds. You also dreamed about walking on the clouds and sliding down rainbows with your mother. You saw other people with different star markings on them, and you used to say that sometimes, for a brief moment, you swore you saw a star on the palm of your hand or on your forehead?"

"Yes, but Father, those were just childhood dreams, just my crazy imagination running wild. You and Jeffery told me that every time I brought it up. What is this all about?"

"Sunshine, what I'm trying to tell you is that they were *not* dreams. Those things really happened to you. You had what is called an out-of-body experience. That was the only way for you to see your mother and her side of the family."

I gave my father a strange look and asked, "What in the world are you talking about? Out of body experience? Have you been visiting the royal tents with the King and Queen, partaking of some of their wine? You're not making any sense." I rubbed the side of my father's arm as if to say it's all going to be okay.

He insisted, "I am fine! I've had no wine! You want to know the truth, don't you? You have wanted to know everything? 'No more secrets.' you said. I am trying to tell you everything and most of what I am telling you will be very hard to believe. It is true, it is all the truths about our family, about your mother. Most important, it is all about yourself and the cursed prophesy."

# Chapter 5

Father began explaining everything and what I heard, I could not believe. It just did not make any sense, but Father and Phoebe assured me it was all true.

I knew my mother was not from Xeenoephillia, she was from some far, distant place. When they told me exactly where my mother was from, I couldn't help but laugh, as if they were both crazy.

It sounded even crazier the moment I heard the words come out of my own mouth, "So, you are saying my mother was a STAR, an actual star like ones you see in the sky? You are saying she came down from the sky, in human form. You are saying I, too, am a star? I am some kind of Starchild?"

"They are known as Starlings," Phoebe interjected.

I continued questioning her, "You mean the members of my family are some sort of Star People or 'Starlings?'"

"Sort of," she said. "Your mother was a Star Being, or Starling, as they like to be called, but your father is completely mortal."

"So I am mortal, too, like my father." I hoped they would tell me I was also normal, so I pressed on, "I can hurt and bleed like my father. I can feel as he can. I surly will die just as he will. Right? None of what you are saying is making any sense."

Father sweetly put his hand on my cheek and said, "Sunshine, look at me." I slowly turned my head towards him with tears of confusion in my eyes. "Yes, you can bleed and hurt and feel just like me, but when it comes to dying, I can only have one life. I can die only once. You, however, can come back from death five times, like the five points on a star. The white streak in your hair shows me what I feared the most, and have been trying to protect you from since you were born, has happened. You, my sweetheart, have died once already."

"So let me get this straight," I said, as I hopped off the bed, turned to face them and tried to pull myself together. "I look and feel like a mortal human, but I am some kind of Star Being, or Starling, you called it. So was my mother. Being this Star creature or whatever I am, I can die and come back to life five times." I said this shaking my head in disbelief.

Phoebe explained, "Yes you can, and when you do come back, it shows by the white glittery streak in your hair. As you can see by this streak, you did, in fact, die when that arrow struck you while you and your friends went to find Cozmo the Owl. It must have had poison in it."

"If that is true," I said with surprising realization, "when Mother died, giving birth to me, I took away her last life." I began crying as I said and felt those words.

Father reassured me, saying, "Murranda, sweetheart, her death was not your fault. You were her greatest gift. She knew what she was doing and what she had to give up. She would have freely given all her lives to have you."

He hugged me and I looked down at my locket with the picture of my mother. That is when I first noticed the stands of white in her hair. How could I have missed it? I then remembered a dream I had about my mother and father. It had felt more like a vision than a dream.

I looked at my father and asked, "Did my mother have any special powers? I mean if she was not mortal like you, Father, could she do certain magical things?"

"What are you asking sweetheart?"

"I had a dream that you and Mother were in this very room and arguing about her going out with the prince. You didn't want her to go with him, but she assured you that all would be okay. You could not do anything to stop her. Then she kissed you on your forehead and you fell into a deep sleep. She created a cloud to catch you and float you to the bed."

"It wasn't just a dream was it, Father? I was reliving what happened, many years ago, between you and Mother, the last time the two of you were here. She had the power to put people into a deep hypnotic sleep and to conjure things."

"Is that true? Can I do the same thing? Earlier, with the prince, I was outside near a ghostly waterfall. Everything was so intense and confusing and I just wanted to escape. Before I knew it, in a blink of an eye, I was here in my room. How could that happen? Did I do that?"

Father cradled me with trembling hands. "Yes, like your mother, you have certain gifts and abilities. I don't know all of them, but she was able to put people into deep hypnotic sleep and conjure things."

He said gently, "I can see this is a lot to take in. I wish you didn't have to hear it, but you wanted to know, and in your own words, you needed to know the truth. So I am trying to tell you just that, everything I know about your mother and what she and you can do, such as the ability to transport yourself in a flash."

"There is so much more, and some things about your abilities I don't even know. But as promised, my Sunshine, no more secrets. Just know this, and it is something I have feared since you were born, once you know the complete truth about who you really are, and what you can do, your life will never be the same again."

With that, Father started to explain everything, but what I was hearing was so difficult to believe. It didn't make sense but Father and Phoebe assured me it was all true. It sounded so preposterous, in part, that I thought they had to be making it up.

They were crazy, or maybe I was, when I heard the words come out of my mouth, "My mother was a Star? I am half-star, half-human? This just can't be."

Phoebe tried to calm me, "Your father is human, so yes, you can bleed and hurt like a human and die like one. Yet because of your mother, you have five lives. On the fifth life, you will die and not come back again."

Father sweetly put his hand on my cheek, "Sunshine, look at me." I slowly turned my head toward him with tears of confusion in my eyes.

"This is everything I have been trying to protect you from," Father said. "I knew you were not ready to handle the truth, but you wanted to know the truth and it should come from me."

"This strand of white hair," he said, as his fingers twirled my white strand of hair, "confirms that you have died once already, so you now have only four lives left. That is one reason I want so desperately to bring you back home so you can live out your lives for a very long time."

I hopped off the bed, faced them and tried to pull myself together. Everything I was hearing was so impossible, I had to ask again, "Let me get this straight. I look and feel mortal, but I am some kind of Star Being and so was my mother. Being this Star creature or whatever I am, means I can die and come back to life five times, or now four more times?"

"Yes you can, and when you do come back it shows with the white strand of hair," Phoebe reiterated.

With a surprising realization in my voice, I said, "If that is true, when my mother died giving birth to me that was her last life." I could feel the sadness in my own voice.

"Please, Murranda, let's go back home where I know you will be safe and away from all of this. I promise to sit down with you and tell you everything," Father pleaded with me.

He said, "You can even bring Glitz with you and your other friends. We will tell you all we know concerning you, your mother, and the Prophesy. Please, Sunshine, just forget about this journey you want to go on. Let me take you home."

"Father, I understand what you and Phoebe are trying to do," I said, as I composed myself and took my father's hand, "but I am staying here for the celebration and the Ball. Nothing will happen to me during the Weekend of Peace. After it is all over and everyone leaves, then I will decide what I will do next. Plus, while I am here, I may find out more about this Prophesy."

66

While Father and I debated whether I would stay or leave the celebration, Deanna, Glitz, and Flutter barged into my room. Immediately, they and started rambling about all that had taken place in the arena earlier, and what happened to Phoenix. They rambled on and on about how Phoenix turned into a huge dragon.

"I knew we couldn't trust her. I knew there was something not right about her," Glitz exclaimed.

Flutter tried to calm him down by signing, "Now, now Glitz. Yes, she somehow turned into that huge dragon, but it does not prove she is evil, just different. Plus, there are known to be some dragons that are friendly. You should know that. We have come across many of them."

"Flutter is right, Glitz," Deanna said. "I saw Phoenix's eyes after she transformed and I think she was just as shocked to suddenly become such a creature, as we all watched her do so. We just need to know where she went. She was following those other dragons from the arena."

"And we also need to know if Jett is going to catch up with her, and if he is going to be safe, once he does," Glitz interrupted.

"I truly don't think she is dangerous," Flutter said.

I walked to Glitz, Deanna, and Flutter, stepped among them, and yelled, "Can you guys stop for a minute? What are you rambling about? What happened to Phoenix? Where did she and Jett go? Where is his sister, Nessa?"

As he entered my room, Jeffery informed us, "Nessa is with some native girl who is supposed to train her in using her new gifts. Nessa found out she can control the elements and this native girl is supposed to be a master at it, so she is training Nessa." Jeffery still clutched Father's Murry Rose. To me, he said, "It is good to see that you are okay, my lady. We were worried," He gently kissed my head.

Deanna looked around my room and could sense something had been occurring before they barged in. She looked at Phoebe and the look

Phoebe gave Deanna puzzled me. It was as if they were talking to each other without moving their lips.

I also noticed that every time Father looked at her, and walked toward her, Deanna would turn away, as if she was afraid of him for some reason. She was the same way around Jeffery, too. I could not help but wonder why she was so aloof and distant around them.

It wasn't as though she was shy, I reasoned, but I could not worry about that right now. I had more than enough to deal with just processing what Father and Phoebe told me about my mother and me. Now I heard a friend turned into a phoenix dragon and flew off, with another friend following her to who knows where.

There was a knock at the door. "Now who could be wanting in my room?" I said as I opened the door. There stood two young girls with wavy brown hair, pale skin, and strange red and gold eyes. They both wore white dresses trimmed in dark red.

"We are here to inform and invite you to the yearly Masquerade Ball that will begin in four hours. His Majesty, the Prince, wanted us to tell you, Lady Murranda, he will pick you up in three hours for a private dinner before the Ball. For the rest of you, dinner will be brought to your rooms." They spoke simultaneously. It was unnerving.

Father quickly moved between me and the girls. He said, abruptly, "You can tell your blood-sucking master…"

The girls hissed at him and showed that they also were blood suckers. Father continued, "Tell your prince that my daughter will have nothing to do with him. So he can eat alone. In fact we were just about to leave this castle and the celebration."

"Now, Father," I said as I pulled him away from the door and the girls, before someone got hurt. "As I told you before, I AM going to my first Masquerade Ball and the Prince WILL be my escort. This is still the Weekend of Peace, so no harm will come to me. I am staying in the castle for the whole celebration, Father. You and Jeffery can leave if you wish, and when I do return home we can then continue our conversation."

I continued stating my plans, "My return home will be when I am ready. I still feel there is something I need to find, so my journey is far from over."

Dismissing everyone in my room, I said "Now, if you all don't mind, I need some time to sort through everything you and Phoebe have told me, and also this news about Phoenix and Jett. I am sure the girls will show you and Jeffery to your rooms. I hear they put you both next door to the King and Queen of our land, and His Majesty has been asking about you. I just need time to myself to sort things out and get ready for my first Ball. I am really looking forward to it."

I then turned to the girls, saying, "Please tell the Prince I will see him in three hours. Now everyone else please leave my room so I can get ready."

"But Murranda dear," Father said. "Please I beg of you let's just…"

Then Jeffery grabbed Father's arm to stop him and said, "Sir, your daughter is right. Nothing bad will happen to her while the celebration is still going on. Let her attend her first Ball. Let us all retire to our rooms until it's time for the Ball."

Everyone left, except Sky. After the others had gone, I walked to my bed, where Sky awaited me at the foot of the bed. I sat down and Sky crawled onto my lap.

He asked, "Are you okay Murry?" He began to purr as I scratched behind his ear. He said, "What's next Murry? Now that you are finding out more and more about yourself and your family could this be what you have been searching for? Is this what your journey is about?"

"I'm not sure, but all I do know, Sky, is that everything I thought I knew has not been so, and a part of me wishes I didn't know all the things I know now. I feel that my life may never be the same again because of everything I've learned."

# CHAPTER 6

While everything unfolded in Murranda's room, Pheonna was in her chambers, watching all of it through the huge, magic crystal floating in the center of her room.

She mused, "So it seems my dear sister and Sir Rudy felt it necessary to tell that little brat the truth about herself and her mother."

As she spoke, she reached to her table of potions and grabbed a dark planter that was filled with soil. She then laid the "Murry Seed" she had taken took from Murry's chamber into the pot.

"The Ball will be starting soon and this flower must be ready in order for my plan to work." She then waved her right hand in the air and a dark fairy appeared.

"How can I help you Sorceress?" The fairy asked.

"I need you to care for this plant. I need the rose to be ready in time for the Ball."

The dark fairy clutched the pot, suspended it in the air and made it start spinning. As the pot spun, she created a rain cloud over it and made the rain cloud drop eight drops of water into it. Then the cloud broke apart into dark, colored crystals that also fell into the pot. As the crystals fell deep into the soil, the rose began to grow. Once the rose appeared, Pheonna and the dark fairy could observe the dark shadow of Murranda, getting ready for the Ball.

"YES!" Pheonna said. "Grow, my little rose. Grow and show me what you know. Hmm…, I see our little Murranda is getting ready for her first Ball. I will be sure to make this a night she will never forget."

The dark fairy gently passed the flower pot back to Pheonna's waiting hands, saying, and "Is there anything else I can do for you?"

"No, that shall be all," Pheonna said. "No! Wait! Can you please summon my Spider Vamps?"

"As you wish."

As soon as the fairy disappeared the Spider Vamp sisters appeared.

The girls quickly looked around, puzzled at first, but quickly knew where they were. They turned towards the sorceress.

"What do you need of us Your Evilness?" Emily asked. "Oh look, sis. She has one of those roses, like the one her sister, Murranda's father, and her friends have."

Looking at Pheonna, Emily said, "But how did you get your hands on one? How did you get it to grow so fast?"

"Idiot!" Jezz said, as she smacked her sister on the back of her head. "She had one of the dark fairies grow it for her."

"Well at least someone was able to do what I wanted them to do." Pheonna replied furiously.

"And what is that supposed to mean?" Jezz interrupted. "You wanted us to expose that crazy, fiery Phoenix for what she truly was, and have that sexy little elf follow her, even though I had better plans for that Elf."

Jezz looked out the window, rubbing her hands together, and continued, "So what are you complaining about? We did just what you asked."

Pheonna replied, "Yes, the elf did go after her like I wanted, but I also wanted his sister elf to go with him. I don't need that little elf getting in my way, now that I know what she can do. The fact that she is so close to Murranda means I need her to get out my way. So I am going to give you two another chance. Go and spy on the female elf. See how her training is coming, and report back to me if there is something I should be worried about."

The Spider Vamps were about to transform into their spider forms, but just as they began to web themselves, Pheonna stopped them.

"I'd rather you go out my chamber door." she said, "As you leave, tell my guards to bring me Captain Darrell, the Pirate. Besides, I am getting tired of your webs all over my floor."

"Well, you created us," giggled Emily as she and Jezz walked out the door, then told the guards to go get the pirate captain.

When they were gone, Pheonna started to pace back and forth, thinking and plotting what she needed to do to get rid of Murranda. At the same time, she could not let anyone know she was behind it. She also needed to find a way to get the prince to fall in love with her, instead of Murranda, and make her queen of the Shadow Land.

"This plan of mine has to work. These smelly moronic pirates have to get that brat out of this castle, out of the Shadow Land, and far away from Xeenoephillia. They have to get her onto their ship and sail far away from here."

Pheonna rambled as she continued pacing, "Before all that can happen, I have to master the illusion spell. I need to become Murranda. I need something of hers, such as hair or blood, for this spell to work correctly, but I have nothing of hers here. Or do I?"

She quickly looked at the Murry Rose, then walked to it and gently rubbed one of its petals.

"Hmm, if I just took one of these petals,

would the rose still thrive? Would it still work, since it is connected to her by the shadow?"

Pheonna pulled one petal from the rose and saw that the rose remained intact.

"Well, the rose is still alive. Now let's see if this petal will allow me to complete the spell."

She walked to the center of her room, where there stood a smoky cauldron. Beside it was a table covered with different types of bottles, herbs, animal parts, and candles, as well as her book of dark magic. She opened the book, read a page of spells then started pouring the contents of different bottles and jars into the smoky cauldron.

She added a cat's tail and a bird's claw with different herbs, then took a dagger that lay next to her book and sliced the palm of her left hand. She clenched her hand into a fist and held it over the cauldron, letting the blood drip down into the mixture.

"Now the final ingredient for this spell," she said to herself as she dropped the rose petal into the smoky pot. Once it was finished, she took a ladle, dipped some of the potion and sipped from it. She placed the ladle back into the pot, then ran both her hands across her face and down the back of her neck. When she did that she turned into the young Murranda.

She asked herself, "Did it work?" She quickly walked to her mirror and saw the young girl she despised looking back at her.

"Perfect! It worked!" She gave an evil laugh when she heard her words spoken in Murranda's voice. She returned to the cauldron and filled a vile with the potion. She put it in her pocket and went back to her mirror to admire her work.

Suddenly, there was a knock at her door and a rugged voice came from the other side, "I be told ye be asking for me fair lady."

Pheonna shook her head until she returned to her evil self. With a flick of her hand, she quickly hid the rose. She cleared her voice to make sure it was her own and said, "Yes Captain. Please come in."

Captain Darrell entered her room with a smug yet alluring look. "How can I be of assistance? Maybe fix us a drink of rum. Or help you off with this?" He grabbed a string off the front of her dress and started to slowly pull it.

Pheonna rolled her eyes in disbelief of what he was trying to do and said, "As tempting as that sounds, Captain, we have some business to discuss, if you and your crew are still wanting any more of those golden swords."

His eyes gleamed with excitement at the mere mention of gold. It is a well known fact that besides the pirate's love for the open sea and rum, his next true love is gold, gems, and diamonds. As soon as she mentioned golden swords he held the one she gave him tightly by his side and started salivating with the thought of more gold.

Pheonna led the captain to a long table overlooking a window that faced the prince's chamber. With a wave of her hands, she magically transformed the top of her table into a miniature Masquerade Ball with tiny little guests in their costumes. The captain was a little shocked and taken aback. He didn't quite know what to think or how to act when he saw the tiny people dance across the table. He reached down to poke at one of them but when he did, his finger just went straight through and caused smoke. The captain shook his head in disbelief.

"Are you quite finished playing around? Can we please get back to my plan of how to get rid of the brat, I mean Murranda?" Pheonna slapped the back of the captain's head as she spoke, in order to get his attention.

She then leaned in and whispered in his ear, "You do want to get to Dragon Island don't you? You want to collect the rest of the golden weapons I have waiting for you there, don't you, my strong and ruggedly handsome captain?"

He looked at her and they both laughed at what was about to take place. The two of them schemed and plotted a plan to get rid of Murranda, or at least get her far away from the prince.

# CHAPTER 7

On the other side of the castle, the young female elf, Nessa, was with her new friend, the young native girl, Serena. The two shared the same gift of controlling and manipulating the elements. Serena was teaching Nessa how to move water from one area to another and then make a strong wall of the water. She also showed Nessa how to cast illusions out of the elements, such as using fire and water to appear as a fiery dragon coming through the water wall. Serena also showed Nessa how to turn a small, glowing candle into a wall of fire, how to create a dancing fire fairy, and how to make rain, then snow, and then a tiny whirlwind.

"See, you are getting it," Serena said.

Nessa started by making three pieces of paper float in midair, then making them go round and round, starting a small whirlwind that got bigger and bigger. The bigger it got, the more excited Nessa became, which made the whirlwind go out of control and become a small tornado.

"What's happening, Serena? I can't stop it!" Nessa cried in fear.

"Okay, okay, Nessa. You need to calm down and try to focus on your breathing and the pattern of the wind. Start pulling your hands back and closer together. Your powers also come from your emotions, so try to stay calm. Concentrate on making the patterns of the wind smaller and smaller."

Once Nessa began to calm down and get control of her emotions, she was able to focus on the wind patterns and make those patterns move slower and slower, until only the three pieces of paper were spinning in a small circle. With her right hand, she snatched the pieces up and yelled with excitement, "I DID IT!"

"I knew you could." Serena said, "Now that you can control your gift you can use the elements at your will, even in battle."

"In battle? How?" Nessa asked.

Serena walked to a running fountain and, with a wave of her hand, the water followed her as she continued walking away from Nessa. Then she turned around and stuck out her arms. The water quickly formed into a giant trident. She threw it at Nessa and it carried her across the room and stopped at a wall, pinning her in midair.

"Okay, now I see. Very impressive," Nessa said. "Now will you let me down please?"

With a twist of her wrist, Serena turned the trident shaped water into steam, and Nessa came sliding down the wall.

"Despite how great my powers are becoming, and the fact I am now able to control them and do some powerful things, I still could not help my brother when he needed my help. Now he is off chasing Phoenix, not knowing if she is the same Phoenix she was before she changed into that huge fiery creature."

Nessa teared up as she walked to the window and looked out, wishing for her brother's safe return.

While Nessa continued to practice and train, everyone else in the castle was getting ready for the big Masquerade Ball.

In the air, somewhere between Xeenoephillia and the remote Dragon Island, a confused and frightened, yet curious Phoenix, in the form of a huge phoenix dragon, followed the two dragons from the arena. One of the dragons was blue like the ocean and the other was red like fire and blood. The red one did not have flames coming from its wings and tail like Phoenix did. During the competition when she and her beloved Jett went up against the Spider Vamp sisters, Phoenix had somehow transformed into a fiery dragon.

Phoenix had many mixed emotions stirring inside her as she soared over the remote island. She looked at her huge fiery wings and long fiery tail and wondered if she would be able to turn back to her human self. Would she see her friends again? Would they be scared of what she had become?

At the same time she was felt frightened and confused, she also felt surprisingly free and exhilarated, neither of which she had ever felt before.

As she followed the two dragons, they took her to an enormous cave in the center of the island. It looked like it was connected to a volcano. What really surprised Phoenix was when they entered the cave, the inside seemed to be its own city or village. There were cave homes inside the cave, a town square, and even a building that looked like a castle.

When they reached the center of the cave in the village square, the blue dragon suddenly changed into a female elf. Then the larger, dark red dragon landed beside the elf but kept its dragon form.

"Let me guess," the dark red dragon chuckled, "you're wondering if you can ever turn back into your human form. As my sister has shown you, you can. As for myself, I prefer to stay like this. I think I look better."

"Better than what is the question," the young elf replied, rolling her eyes. "Brother dear, let's not frighten our soon-to-be-queen. Now that we have finally found her, can't you see she doesn't really know who she is?"

Addressing Phoenix, the young elf said, "Please, Your Highness, forgive my brother. He means well. Yes, you can change from your human form, or in my case, elf form, to dragon and back again. Just calm your emotions and focus on what your human form is."

So Phoenix did just that and slowly began transforming to her normal self.

The young elf looked at her brother, still in his dragon form, and hit him in his large scaly leg to persuade him to transform as they had done. In reply, he just rolled his eyes, shook his head, jumped up and spun around, and turned into his human self.

The two elves looked very much alike. There was no mistaking they were related, except she had elf ears and he had human ears. They were both well built with olive-toned skin, dark black hair and blue eyes.

Her hair was longer, with some blue streaks in it, while her brother had shoulder length hair with dark red streaks. Both wore a type of armor that appeared to be glued or painted on them. Hers was silver and blue with a blue dragon design on the chest plate. His was gold and red with a red dragon on the chest plate.

"Forgive our rudeness, Your Highness," the young male said. "I am Drake and this is my sister Rayne. We are the Agent Guardians of Dragon Island and the Protectors of the Royal Dragons, meaning you, Your Highness, and your family."

Stunned and confused, Phoenix asked, "What is all this 'Your Highness' talk the two of you keep calling me? I grew up as an orphan. A gypsy family took me in and raised me. So how can I be of royal birth?"

"But you are, Your Highness," Rayne quickly interrupted. "You come from a long line of royal blood. The reason this all seems so hard to believe is because when you were born you were sent far away for your own safety. Then, our island was being invaded by Vikings and pirates, who wanted to destroy or enslave us. We knew, one day after the Vikings and Pirates left our island home, you would come of age and return to us to reclaim your rightful place as our new queen."

Rayne continued, "We knew you would bring us back to the way we once were, a strong and proud race of dragons. When my brother and I saw you fighting those Spider Vamps in the arena, we could tell you were just coming into your powers. That's when we both knew we needed to lead you here and prepare you to take your rightful place on Dragon Island."

"Wait a minute!" Phoenix laughed. "You two are Agent Guardians? You look to be my age or younger, which is young, because I've been aging somewhat rapidly since I left the gypsy fair. I'm not sure how or why I am doing that."

"Now that you've come into your powers, and have done your first transformation, your aging will slow down drastically. For example, my brother and I are over 550 years old," Rayne told her.

But, we will explain more about that later," interrupted Drake. "My sister is forgetting that we need to take you to Her Majesty's chambers. She needs to see you."

"So, if I'm Your Highness and she is Her Majesty, that means I am about to meet my mother, my birth mother. The one who abandoned me all those years ago."

"She did not abandon you. She did what had to be done to protect you," Rayne explained, putting her arms around Phoenix and leading her into the chamber of dragons and to the queen's room.

Phoenix began thinking about her beloved Jett, the forest elf, and how he was trying to follow her. Then she thought about her other friends at the Dark Castle in the Shadow Land, and about the big Masquerade Ball about to take place.

"Wait!" She yelled. "I need to go back to Xeenoephillia, to the Dark Castle. My friends are there and I am sure they are wondering what has happened to me."

"First you are to come with us to your family," Drake insisted. "We can worry about them and deal with your friends later." He shook his head in disapproval.

"Fine, I'll do what you say for now," Phoenix said reluctantly. "But after that I must get back to my friends and keep a promise I made to someone."

The three of them walked down the dark chamber hallway and with each step they took torches on each side of the hallway lit up. Ancient drawings of dragons with different features, shapes and sizes were on the walls. Some of the dragons looked like them and some looked as though they were in water. Some drawings were of small dragons wrapped around limbs or branches of some type. There were even drawings of dragon eggs and hatchlings. Some young ones were born as dragons, while others looked more human or elf-like and had scales and feathers on their faces, heads and arms.

"As you can see, Phoenix," Rayne explained, "we come from a long line of dragons that date back for centuries. We come in all shapes and sizes, colors and types. Some are good and get along well with humans, elves and other creatures."

"On the other hand, some of us feel we are above mere mortals and would prefer the world would be rid of them. If that makes us evil, so be it," Drake chimed in proudly and boastfully, which confused and frightened Phoenix somewhat.

"Excuse my obnoxious brother," said Rayne, shaking her head and trying to calm her brother. "I myself, as well as your parents, think we can work together with mortals."

"Is that where you are taking me now, to meet my parents?" Phoenix asked.

"Your father died in battle, protecting you and Dragon Island, but your mother remains alive. She has been mourning your father's death for years and has also been mourning for you and hoping for your safety," Rayne explained.

"Mourning for me? She sent me away to protect me. Why mourn for me? I'm not dead."

"True," Rayne said, "but she didn't know when or if she would ever see you again. Now that you are here, your mother and all of us on the island have hope that we can restore our beloved home to the way it was before."

"I understand what you are trying to tell me, Rayne, but I cannot stay here and be your new queen. I have family and friends who need me," Phoenix tried to explain.

"Will you at least come and meet your mother? Let her know you are still alive and safe. Then explain to her your new life. Maybe we can find a way for you to have both."

Phoenix nodded her agreement and the three of them entered another room. There, by a huge, open window, stood a woman with long, white hair and fair skin. She was wearing a black and gray dress with a long train.

"Your Majesty!" Drake announced. "We have someone here you need to meet. She has come a long way to see you, My Queen."

"Oh, Drake," the woman said with a majestic, yet very sad, tearful voice, "please give our guest my apologies. I am in no mood to see or entertain anyone right now, not on the anniversary of the night I lost my husband and only daughter. Please make sure our guest is well-fed and rested from his long journey, then send him on his way."

Rayne gave Phoenix a slight nudge and whispered, "Please say something to her."

Phoenix reluctantly approached the queen and said, "I am sorry you are so sad, but you no longer have to feel that way. Your daughter has grown up to be very independent and strong. She has come here to thank you for saving her life, I mean my life."

The queen could not believe what she was hearing. She turned around slowly and looked into Phoenix's eyes, then asked, "Is it really you? My child has come back to me. You have come home."

She placed her hands on Phoenix's face then embraced her. "Well maybe not a child anymore, but all the same, you have come home to me. So what do they call you? Where have you been all these years? When you were born we were not able to have the naming ceremony because we were under attack by the Vikings and pirates."

"My name is Phoenix."

The queen studied her and said, "With those markings on your face and body, I can see why that is what you are called. I am known as Queen Phazha, but of course you can call me Mother."

"Well," Phoenix said as she stepped back. "That may be difficult for me to do, since I don't really know you. For now, may I just call you Phazha?"

"Oh yes, of course you can," she said, clearing the lump in her throat. "We'll have plenty of time to get to know each other, now that you are home to stay."

Phazha ordered, "Drake, you and your sister announce to everyone we will have a banquet to welcome home my daughter and Dragon Island's future queen."

"WAIT!" Phoenix yelled. "I did not agree to stay and rule an island. I don't care who I am supposed to be."

"But it's your des…" Drake tried to say until his sister stopped him.

"SSShhh! This is between them."

Phoenix continued, "I have a life, a wonderful life in Xeenoephillia. I just came here because of what happened to me during the Weekend of Peace tournament when somehow I turned into a huge, fiery phoenix-dragon. Then I met these two and they had me follow them here so they could explain what had just happened to me."

Phoenix continued to explain, "It was then I heard about a royal family which I belong to. Rayne and Drake told me I am no longer with my real family because of the war here. My family had to send me away to protect me. Now I am to come to you, to let you know I am safe and alive, and to thank you for saving me."

She concluded, "So I agreed to meet you and let you see that I am fine and doing well. Yes, I do want to know more about who and what I am, but right now I need to get back to my friends and the Weekend of Peace celebration."

The queen replied, "Oh yes, the Weekend of Peace celebration in your land. I know about that. Before you were born, your father and I attended it. I remember a young gypsy named Phoebe, back then. She was the one who helped your father and me to get you to a safe place. May I come with you? I want to find her and thank her for protecting you all these years."

"But, Your Majesty, are you sure you can make such a long journey? You have not taken flight for many years," Drake exclaimed.

"I appreciate your concern, Drake, but I am more then capable of flying. I may be old but my wings still have some flight in them."

She stated proudly, "Plus, as Phoenix's mother, I should be the one to train her in her new role and teach her more about who she is, what she can do and how to control her new powers. Most importantly, I want to get to know all about my daughter."

Phoenix looked at Phazha and felt something she had never felt before, but had always wished for, a mother's love. She smiled at the queen as if to say, yes, come with me.

Her mother looked at her and said, "Phoenix my dear, I'll come only if you do not object. Before you go back to your friends, we must follow custom and make a formal announcement to our people that you have returned and are safe. It will give them hope that soon we can return Dragon Island to the way it used to be."

Phoenix agreed, so she, Queen Phazha, Drake and Rayne, stepped out onto the balcony overlooking the square.

The queen walked to the balcony's edge and surveyed her people gathered around the square. A thunderous applause and cheers began to ring out. The queen then raised her hands to silence the excited crowd. She said, "My beloved subjects of

Dragon Island, the moment we all have been waiting for and dreaming of for years has finally come true. My long lost daughter has safely returned to us. Now, hopefully soon, she will take her rightful place as your new queen. But before that can happen, we will be joining some of the Dragon family in Xeenoephillia to celebrate the Weekend of Peace. Once we return, we will have our own grand celebration here for my daughter, your future queen. So let me present to you, Princess Phoenix."

Phoenix became overwhelmed by all the people and could see that some of them were in human or elf form, while others changed into their dragon forms. Some even started breathing out fire, as everyone cheered and cheered at the news.

The little group returned to the queen's chambers to get ready to go to the Dark Castle in the Shadow Land.

Phoenix stepped to Phazha and said, "I'm still not sure if I can be your future queen; I don't even know who or what I am."

"I understand," Queen Phazha replied. "This is all very confusing to you, but the more we get to know each other, the more I can help you understand who you are and all you can do. Who knows, you might find that here is just where you need to be. But there is no pressure."

Phazha suggested, "Let's go to the celebration where your friends are. I believe it is getting close to time for the big Masquerade Ball. So do you have a date for this event my dear?"

Phoenix just turned her head, giggled and blushed.

"By the look on your face, I have to guess you do. So who is he? As your mother I have the right to know, don't I?" They both laughed.

"He is a forest elf named Jett. In fact, I would not be surprised if he isn't looking for me right now. I'm sure he and my other friends are worried about me. So if you don't mind, can we leave now?"

So the queen, Phoenix, Drake, and Rayne stepped outside and as soon as they did, Drake and

Rayne quickly transformed into their dragon forms and hovered over Phoenix and the queen.

Phoenix looked up at them and said, "Okay, how is it that you two can make it look so easy?" She was frustrated as she flapped her arms and jumped up and down.

Drake and Rayne could not help but laugh. "It's not that hard. Just do it." Drake said.

Phazha put her hands on Phoenix's shoulders, saying, "It will all come naturally to you soon my dear but the way we transform is by wanting to, or by emotions."

"Oh, I can understand emotions being a part of it," Phoenix said. "That must be how I transformed the first time, when I got so mad at the Spider Vamp sisters. But when you say I can transform by just wanting it, what does that mean?"

The queen tried to explain, "Just look up at Drake and Rayne, or better yet, think of your friends. Think of your elf friend, Jett, and your feelings for him. Think about how badly you want to get back to him. Now flap your arms and jump up at the same time, and, poof, you have transformed."

As soon as the queen said, "poof," she transformed herself into a silvery white dragon with scales. On her head and tail, she had white shiny feathers. She was beautiful.

Phoenix did as she said and concentrated her thoughts on her friends, but mostly Jett, and how she wanted to be with him and dance with him. She could feel her heart racing. She raised her arms and jumped, transforming into the fiery phoenix dragon.

She screamed, "I did it," startled when fire came out of her mouth with her words.

"I told you that you could do it," Phazha said with such pride in her voice. "Keep practicing and soon it will become as natural as breathing."

She added, "But there is so much more to who we are and what we can do besides just transforming back and forth from dragon to human form. In time, I will show you everything but first let's get to your other family and friends."

So the four of them flew back to Xeenoephillia, back to the Shadow Land and back to the Dark Castle, where Phoenix hoped her beloved Jett was still waiting for her.

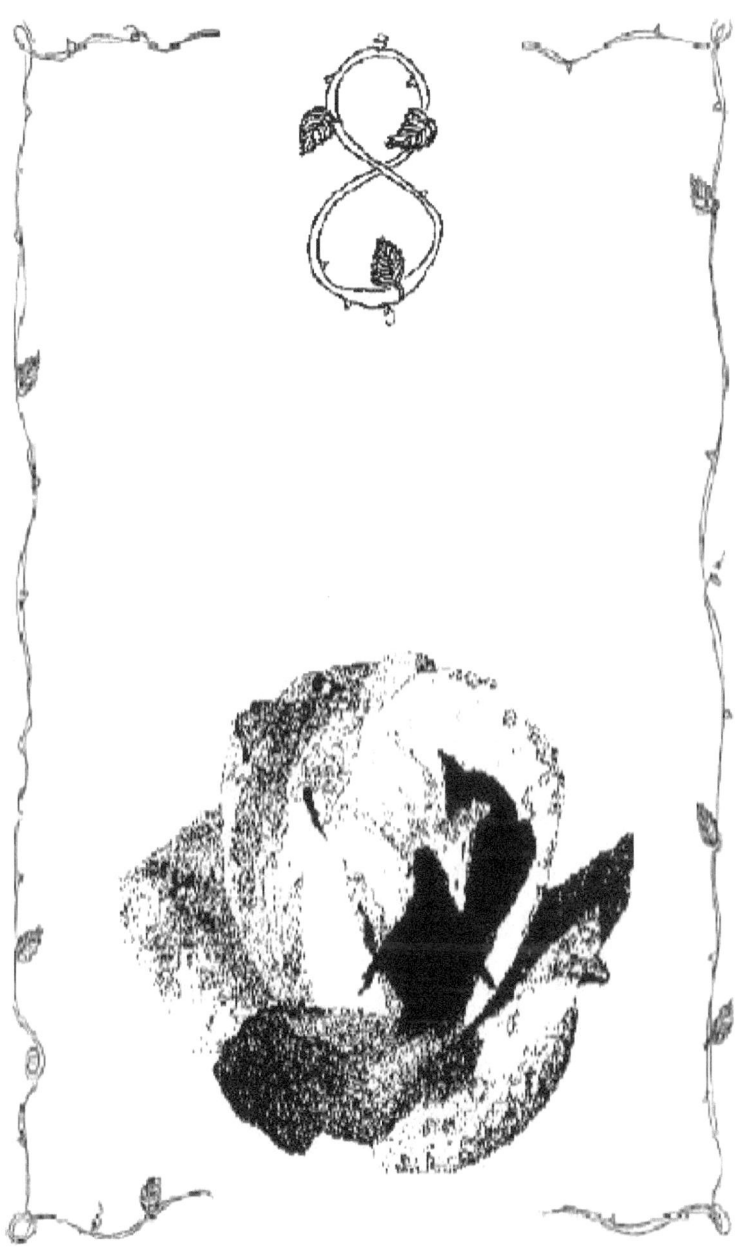

# Chapter 8

Meanwhile, the Shadow Land Weekend of Peace celebration was in its final evening. Everyone was preparing for the famous Masquerade Ball. Jett, the forest elf, had been looking all over the castle and the Shadow Land for Phoenix, but she was nowhere to be found. Jett hit dead end after dead end, refusing to give up.

He ran into his sister, Nessa, and her teacher and new friend, Serena. He noticed how Serena's teaching had really helped Nessa. His little sister was showing great improvements in her new-found gifts.

"Maybe they have seen Phoenix. I hope so," Jett thought to himself as he drew closer to them. With a hopeful smile, he asked, "Have either of you seen Phoenix anywhere?"

"Sorry brother but no, we haven't. The last time we saw her was at the tournament when she changed into that fiery flying beast," Nessa said as she went to hug her brother.

"I saw her flying off, following two other dragons. I'm not sure where they flew off to," Serena said. "Perhaps they took her to Dragon Island. That is an Island outside of Xeenoephillia."

"I pray not," said Jett. "That is over a five moon journey. I would need a ship to get there and the Ball is tonight. We were supposed to go together. Without her, those Spider Vamp sisters will be all over me."

"I'm sure she knows that, dear brother. I'm sure she will come back by then but how can we be sure she will be the same as she was before she turned? How do we know if she can turn back to her human form? We don't really know her now, do we?" Nessa said as she tried to comfort him.

"I know her, Nessa," Jett said with a strong certainty in his voice. "Who's to say she can't turn back. We have seen these dragons turn back and forth from human to dragon and back. I believe she will also be able to do that."

"That may be true, brother," Nessa said in a concerned voice, "but we have also seen them destroy many villages and homes. So how can we be sure she will still be our friend, now that her true self had surfaced?"

"Now Nessa," Serena interrupted, "not all dragons are evil. In my village, we have worked well with many kinds of friendly dragons who have helped bring water to a dry and thirsty village. They've also helped by bringing heat and warmth to a freezing family. So there is an excellent chance your Phoenix will stay the same as she has been, a good hearted person."

"I agree with Serena," said Jett. "Just because she has changed physically does not mean her heart has changed. She is still the same Phoenix. I just know it."

Jett shifted his thoughts and said, "Putting that aside, sister, I want to tell you that I noticed Serena has really helped you master your gifts. Our brother, Evanwood, would be so proud of you."

"I couldn't have done it without her teaching," said Nessa, "but what are you going to do if you can't find Phoenix? You know, once those

Spider Vamps find out you are not with her, they are going to be up to their tricks trying to get to you, especially that Jezz. She really has her eyes set on you." Nessa looked over at Serena and they both giggled.

Just as Nessa said her name, Jezz, in her spider form, crawled out of a crack in a nearby tree. Jezz, the older of the two sisters, used her web to descend and begin forming her vampire shaped cocoon.

After it formed, the top of the webbed cocoon started to expose her vampire self. She giggled, seductively and evilly, saying, "Now, are you three talking about little ole me? Did I hear that your poor, fiery friend flew away and left my sexy elf alone?"

Before her web could finish unraveling, Nessa quickly formed a small rain cloud. With a flick of her fingers, she made the rain cloud pour over Jezz, making her web so sticky that it clung to her, trapping her in her own web. She could not even move her arms to get back at them.

"How dare you! Get me out of this now or so help me..." Then Jezz aimed and tried to spit web from her mouth toward Nessa but Nessa used her breath to change the wind pattern. The web that was heading straight to her shot back at Jezz and went into the small rain cloud. It landed right across Jazz's mouth so that she couldn't speak.

Serena, Jett, and Nessa laughed in astonishment.

"Wow sister dear, you do have a handle on your new gifts," Jett said as he put his arms around Nessa and Serena.

"Yes, I have to agree with you Jett. My work seems to be done here. You don't need my help anymore," Serena said with pride.

Nessa smiled and said, "Thank you. Now let's leave Jezz to her own mess and go get ready for the Ball. I'm sure we will find Phoenix before it begins."

Just then, Jezz's sister, Emily, came out of the same tree and looked at what they had done to her sister "What happened to you sister?" she asked telepathically.

"It was that little forest twit and her new abilities," Jezz yelled back at her telepathically. "Now help me get out of this so I can go get that elf and take her brother for my own, now that his fiery dragon friend has flown away."

"But, sister dear," Emily interrupted, "you can have your revenge later. I was told to come get you. Our prince wants us for something."

Since the Dark Prince's blood runs through all the vampires, they can never say no to his commands. They are all somehow seared to the prince and his family.

Reluctantly, Jezz brushed all the sticky web off, transformed back into her spider self, and followed her sister to the castle and the prince's chambers.

# Chapter 9

The challenges, games and events are now finished and everyone in the dark castle is slowly getting ready for the lavish Masquerade Ball. The castle's servants are on hand to assist the guests in any way, while other servants are preparing the grand Ballroom and the rest of the castle for the event.

We find our troubled Prince Demitri pacing the castle hallways. As he paces, he looks at all the family portraits on the wall, noting they seem to be looking back at him, feeling what he feels, but also knowing what needs to be done.

In their own way the portraits are alive. They talk among themselves about how the prince needs to go forward with the Prophesy before it is too late. From her portrait, his mother looks down and reaches out to him with a worried, yet loving, expression. She looks at him as if to say, "You know what needs to be done, my son."

He looks up at her, shakes his head and says, "I know, Mother. If I don't go through with the Prophesy we cannot take over all of Xeenoephillia. Without her blood, we are all confined here in the Shadow Land."

"Yes, Son, and with her blood you can finally walk in the light. Then the two of you can create more day-walkers and take back what is rightfully ours." His mother's voice echoed the halls.

"There has to be another way. Must I truly do this? She doesn't even know who or what she is."

Just then the ghostly form of a woman appeared, floating next to the prince. She placed one arm around his shoulder and moaned, "My poor, dear Demitri. I can see you are having feelings for this creature. She is just like her mother, but unfortunately, you were not able to take her mother as previously planned. Now you must take her daughter. Demitri it is time our people stop living in the shadows."

"The Prophesy states that once we take control of the Star, and make her one of us, we can then break through the shadows and walk in the sun," the ghostly woman explained.

"Then," she added, "Xeenoephillia can finally be ours, but, she must be willing to give herself to you in order for this work. If not, you must take her and drain her of her light. Then all of Xeenoephillia will forever live in Darkness."

The specter said to Demitri, "You must take her as your bride, and by what I hear in these hallways, it seems the two of you are getting very close. You must take her by this night and under the Blood Moon. You must convince her to stay, once the celebration is over. She has to believe she will still be safe in your care, even after the rest of the guests have left, especially her friends and father. They must not stop us again. We are so close."

"Why are you questioning, this, my son? Don't you want to take over more then just the Shadow Land? Don't you want all of Xeenoephillia? In the past all you talked about was having Morinda, her mother. You wanted the Prophesy to come true. You tried everything you could to get her mother to fall for you. Isn't Murranda her mother's daughter? The same blood flows through her, but more importantly, the same light is in her as was in her mother."

"I can still remember you painting portraits of yourself walking in the sun and the beautiful sunrises. Instead of painting those sunrises, wouldn't you rather see one for yourself? Wouldn't you want to live in the sun instead of hiding in the shadows afraid of it burning and killing you? You can, my son, once you take young Murranda for your bride. She has to stay, even after the Weekend of Peace is over."

Demitri replied, "But she doesn't know who she is. Who's to say there are not others out there, other Starlings in our castle? I am sure there is a way we can find them and turn one of them. Does it have to be her?"

Demitri pleaded. "Does it have to be Murranda?"

The ghostly woman commanded, "Yes, my son, it does. Even more so now!" She looked at him and realized what she was saying.

"Why is that?" He looked out of a window facing across at Murranda's room.

"Because I can see you are starting to have feelings for this one. You care for her. I feel that she is unknowingly beginning to feel something for you, as well," she explained as she floated behind him, also looking out the window into Murranda's room.

In a huff, Demitri turned from the window and walked through his ghostly mother, shaking his head and protesting, "I don't know what you are talking about. Feelings? Hah! I just think because she is half mortal that the Prophesy may not be about her. Maybe the Prophesy describes a pure Starling."

His mother asked, "Has anyone ever seen a pure one? A pure Starling could not walk among us. That is why they are Halflings, half-Starling and half of another species, such as mortal like Murranda. Her feelings for you will make it easy for you to make her your bride."

"But the Prophesy also says she has to be willing to become my bride," Demitri explained, walking toward his dresser and slamming his hand on it.

"For her to become my bride, Mother, she has to first become what I am." He slowly looked up at the mirror in front of him, barely seeing his reflection looking back at him.

"Oh, My Son, how long since you have fed last? Your reflection is almost no more."

His mother pointed to his door with her ghostly finger. There was a knock, and when it opened, a woman in a long, black dress walked in. She was in a trance-like state and had several bite marks on her neck and arms.

"You need to feed on her and remain strong," Demitri's mother said. "We are so close to having what we deserve. This is not the time for you to weaken yourself."

The woman in black walked to the prince, brushing her hair to one side and exposing her neck to him. As he stared at her bare neck and veins, he saw the blood rushing through them.

He could not help but think, Could he truly turn Murranda into what he was? How could he take what she had and he always wanted, mortality, humanity and pure innocence?

My life is not a life I would wish on anyone, he thought to himself. He took a bite from the woman's neck and fed from her, not enough to kill her but just enough so his reflection would return in the mirror.

Just then, two black widow spiders crawled out from under the prince's door and, with their webs, quickly transformed themselves into the Spider Vamp sisters. As they were transforming, and before the sisters noticed her, Demitri's ghostly mother quickly floated out and jumped into her portrait.

"You summoned us, Sire?" The sisters spoke simultaneously, grinning at what the prince was doing to the woman in black.

Demitri took his fangs off the woman's neck and quickly retracted them. He looked into the woman's eyes, "Now go to your room and get ready for the Ball. Your date will pick you up and you two will have a wonderful time."

The woman nodded her head, looked at the prince and said, "If there is nothing else you need Sire, I must get ready for the Ball."

"No, there is not. You may go now," he said. She turned and walked out the door passing the two sisters.

Jezz stared at her, licking her lip. "As always, our prince has delicious taste," Jezz said with a devilish grin. "I hope she tasted as yummy as she smelled."

"So, you wanted us Sire," Emily interrupted. "How can we serve you?"

"Yes, Emily my dear, I did," he said as he wiped the blood off his lips with a handkerchief. Then with a flick of his fingers he set the handkerchief on fire until it just vanished in smoke.

"As everyone else is preparing the castle for the Ball and helping our guests with whatever they need, I need the two of you to help me with something special I have planned for someone. I want it done before the Ball begins."

He explained, "It is a private dinner for two in my personal gazebo. The chefs are already preparing the meal for us. I need the two of you to decorate the place. I need this night to be an unforgettable night for this person."

"Is this for our sorceress, Pheonna? This is so sweet, Sire." Emily gushed.

"No, my silly child," a voice came from behind her. A dark, bluish fog swirled behind the Spider Vamp sisters and the sorceress herself appeared in a shimmery blue and black gown trimmed in diamonds and sapphires. "This romantic dinner our prince is preparing is not for me, but for his new-found interest, Lady Murranda."

"Oh, the Prophesy, I see!" Jezz added with excitement. "Our prince is getting ready for the Prophesy to happen."

"Getting ready?" Emily questioned," the Blood Moon will not be here until long after the Weekend of Peace celebration is over."

Jezz leaned into her sister and said, "Let's just say, Sister, our prince is going to make this night so unforgettable that the Lady Murranda will not want to leave, even after this weekend comes to an end."

Jezz schemed on, "As soon as the Prophesy is fulfilled, we can take over all of Xeenoephillia and even Elfinnea. Then I can get my hands on that sexy elf."

Emily glared at her sister as Jezz quickly added, "Oh, I meant we can get our hands on him Sister dear." Emily looked away smiling and Jezz just rolled her eyes and chuckled.

"Can we please stop talking about this Prophesy?" Demitri yelled, slamming his hand on his dresser to quiet the conversation. "That is all I have been hearing since I arrived. Only I can decide WHEN and IF this Prophesy will be fulfilled!"

"IF? What do you mean 'IF,' Sire?" Jezz snapped back knowing she could be getting herself into a lot of trouble by yelling at the prince. "If you don't take her by the night of the Blood Moon how can we…"

"ENOUGH!" The prince yelled back. "I don't want to hear any more about any Prophesy," he continued to explain, as he looked over and glared at his mother's portrait on the wall. "If I hear anyone of my subjects or family say another word about any Prophesy, they will answer to me, and trust me when I say, whether or not this is still the Weekend of Peace means nothing to me."

He commanded, "So Emily, Jezz, please do as I asked. Pheonna, my dear, I already have something special for you and Phoebe. I've already had someone send for your sister. You are to meet her near the Ghostly Falls, your favorite place when you two were younger. You are to bring it back to the Ball when the two of you make your entrance. Now go. I'm sure Phoebe is almost there. I will see you both at the Ball."

Demitri walked to Pheonna and kissed her on her forehead as she held back tears of rejection and wished she could be the one having the romantic dinner with him. Demitri then whispered in her ear, "By the way, I've never seen you look lovelier than you do right now. As always, both you and your sister must save me a dance. Now go."

Pheonna slowly looked up and smiled into his eyes, hoping he did not see her start to tear up. She turned and left his room, then went down the hall and out to meet her sister. She stopped at the staircase railing when she heard his door close.

"Hmm, enjoy this magical night with the prince, Murranda, for it will be your last." Pheonna said to herself, clenching tightly to the railing. "As far as the Prophesy, my dear prince, who says it needs to happen for you to take over all of

Xeenoephillia. I may know a way for you to have it all without that little brat, but only when you make ME your bride and we rule it all together."

She laughed as she walked down the stairs and with each step, she turned into dark blue smoke and drifted away to meet her sister at the place the two of them loved as children.

# Chapter 10

I finally have my room to myself, so I begin getting ready for my first Masquerade Ball. Part of me is so excited, as I remember the balls and celebrations my father hosted when I was a young girl. I would sneak down from my room to take a peek, wishing I could be a part of it all, the dancing and laughing. I dreamed of the day I could go to one of these balls. Now here I am, about to attend my very first ball.

In spite of my excitement, I could not help but think about everything I had just learned about my family and myself. I walked around my room, shaking my head and hearing the voices of my Father, Phoebe, and the prince, telling me things that just didn't seem real.

I walked to my vanity table and stared hard in the mirror, looking for something that would confirm all that they had said about me, that I am some kind of Star Child. I pulled the hair away from my forehead to see if the star I thought I saw when I arrived in my room was still there.

Then, I just shook it all off and started to get ready for the Ball. After I finished my bath, I threw on a dark, red robe that was hanging in my bathroom. I walked back and sat down at my vanity table, staring again into the mirror. I looked at the foot of my bed, where Sky was asleep and purring.

I called gently, "Sky, Sky, wake up. Shouldn't you be getting ready for the Ball?"

"Oh, are you sure you'll be okay Murry?" He yawned as he got up stretching and kneading the bed.

"I'll be fine, but I would like some time to myself before the servants come to help me with my dress."

Sky hopped off the bed and headed to his room to get ready. I looked at the night stand by my bed where I had a picture of my mother standing next to my father.

"I really wish you were here, Mother. I need you right now," I cried. "I have so many questions, so many things I don't understand."

I looked back at my vanity mirror, still thinking about all the things everyone had told me about who and what I am, and my mother was. I was so mentally drained that I just needed to lay my head down for a bit, collect my thoughts, and relax a little.

I laid my head across my arms on the vanity table and closed my eyes. Before I knew it, I was in an unexpected dream. I dreamt I was sitting on a fluffy cloud floating up higher and higher into the sky. I looked down and could see the dark castle getting smaller and smaller as I kept ascending.

Then I was surrounded by billions of stars. I could hear the stars giggle and call my name welcoming me back. I then reached a place that was breathtakingly beautiful, a city of clouds and a castle that looked like it was carved out of diamonds. "Where am I?" I thought to myself.

"This is where I am from, My Darling," a voice came from behind me. I knew I'd never heard this voice before, but for some reason I felt as if I should know it.

"Now that you are finding out who you really are, it is time you find out where we first came from," the voice tried to explain.

"Where WE came from?" I quickly questioned, as I turned around to see who was behind me.

There was a very bright light around what appeared to be a slender woman. She started to walk closer to me. I could not believe what I was seeing.

"Mother? Is that really you?" I called out as I woke up and lifted my head from the vanity table. I looked into the mirror and could have sworn I saw my mother standing behind me with her hand on my shoulder.

But it was only half of her. From the waist down it looked as if she was some kind of white horse, almost like a centaur. I quickly turned around and when I did she was gone. All that stood in front of me was Deena, my unicorn friend, all dressed up for the Ball. Her beautiful mane had been braided with tiny white and pink roses. She was wearing a beautiful, glittery mask.

"Are you okay, Murranda? You look as if you've seen a ghost," Deena said with a concerned and strange look in her eyes.

"Yes, I'm okay," I replied, trying to shake the images I just saw, or thought I saw. "You just startled me that's all. You look stunning Deena."

"Thank you. I still think we should just skip the Ball and get out of this castle and away from the prince and the sorceress. Let's continue on with your journey, Murry." She pushed the door wide open with her hoof hoping to get me to leave with her.

"Now, Deena, this is my very first Ball and I am going to attend it with the prince. Nothing bad is going to happen to me during this Weekend of Peace," I explained as I walked over to close the door. Just then, Cozmo the Golden Owl flew into my room in a panic, yelling for us to quickly close the door.

"Murranda please, let's just leave. I'm sure your father will throw you many Grand Balls," Deena pleaded.

"I can't believe I'm saying this," Cozmo replied, as he hopped on top of Deena's head, "but I agree with this one. Let's just get out of this crazy castle."

"Now Cozmo, I can't believe you are agreeing with me," Deena replied with surprise. "Last I saw of you, you were in a room full of servants fanning you, peeling you grapes and feeding you all sorts of stuff. What could have changed your tune?"

Cozmo started cleaning his feathers aggressively and explained, "Let's just say I found out why I am such a prized guest here. It is because they are making me the prize to be given away to the winner of the competition. I need to find that gypsy witch and get her to take back this blasted curse. "

"But Cozmo," I giggled trying to not let him see it, "I thought the only way to break the curse is for you to do a truly selfless act of kindness."

"As I explained before, lassie," he snarled, "I've tried many times to do just that, but every time I look back I am still this feathery fowl."

"Cozmo, a selfless act is doing something for someone without thinking about how it can or will benefit you later."

"Well, me lassie, that is just silly. Why should I do anything for anyone if it is not going to benefit me in some way?"

Deena and I just rolled our eyes in disbelief at what he was saying.

"So, are we ready? Let's fly out of this overgrown bird cage." He flew behind me trying to shoo me out the door with his wings.

I planted my feet down and yelled, "Enough of this! I am staying and I am going to attend this Masquerade Ball with the prince. I am sorry if you don't approve, but I am old enough to make my own decisions. For the LAST TIME, I am going to stay in the castle until the Weekend of Peace celebration has come to an end. Then, and only then, will I decide to leave or not."

"What do you mean or NOT?" Deena asked with concern in her voice.

"Don't worry about that now," I said as I pushed them out of my room. "If the two of you don't mind, I would like to finish getting ready for the Ball. I will see you all there, I'm sure."

I closed the door and turned around to continue getting ready for the Ball. Suddenly a purple smoke started to fill my room. When it cleared, my room was filled with roses and orchids.

There was also a huge gift box on my bed with a big dark red bow. I pulled the bow and opened the box. What I saw took my breath away. It was a gorgeous dark red gown trimmed in black with matching long black silk gloves and a red and gold mask with red, black and gold feathers. There was also a note in the box that read:

*I do hope you find this small gift I have sent to your liking, and may I invite you to a private dinner for two at one of my favorite spots in the castle. My servants will be at your door to assist you in getting ready. Once you are ready, place this black feather on your windowsill for another surprise that will take you where I will be waiting. Until then, my sweet Murranda,*
  *Love*

  *Demitri.*


As I pressed the note and feather tightly against my chest, I could not believe just how sweet this prince was being, even though everyone around me was making him out to be some kind of monster. All I could see was compassion and love. Now I was even more excited about this magical evening.

Just then, there was a knock on the door. A thin plume of purple smoke came from under my door, into my room and formed a thick wall. From the purple wall came a slender female vampire.

"Hello my dear," she said. "Forgive me if I frightened you, but our prince wants me to help you get ready for what he hopes will be an unforgettable night for you. I see the prince's gifts have arrived. Let's do something with your face and hair before we put on your dress."

She clapped her hands and pairs of hands with white gloves came from behind her. There was no body, just white-gloved hands floating in the air. She looked at them and told each of them what to do. I sat down at my vanity table while some of the hands did my eyes and cheeks, others sprayed perfume on me and one did my lips. It was all so unbelievable.

The woman was behind me doing my hair, curling it, twisting some of my hair up on my head, and letting the rest of the curls fall loosely down my neck and shoulders.

She told me how much I looked like my mother and how she had stayed in this very room. She also told me that they had helped my mother get ready for her Ball with the prince. I then looked up and saw the floating hands grab my dress from the box on my bed. It floated over to me as I stood up and then it floated over my head. I took off my robe and raised my arms as the dress fell and draped over me.

"You might want to hold on to something quickly," the woman said. As soon as she said that I could feel the hands grabbing the straps from the back of my dress pulling them tighter and tighter making sure the dress fit perfectly. Then a smaller hand came floating towards me with my mask. After I was completely dressed, the hands gave me a thumbs up and quickly vanished.

The vampire woman just looked at me in astonishment and said, "I truly feel that all eyes are going to be on you tonight, my lady. Now that my work is done here I shall leave you and help the other servants get things ready for the Ball. I believe you are to meet the prince for dinner before the Ball begins." She took the black feather that I had placed on my bed and handed it to me then she too vanished.

Beside my bed was a full-length mirror. I walked to it and spun around. I could not believe what I was seeing. I had never felt so beautiful. I looked down at the black feather I was holding and stroking.

"I wonder what Demitri has in store for me." I walked to my window and laid the feather on the window's edge. A gust of wind took the feather high into the air.

As I watched it float away, I noticed something flying towards me. The closer it got the bigger it became. It was a gigantic black swan. I had never seen such a large swan. When it reached my windowsill, a huge white cloud floated under the swan so he could land on it. I reached out to pet him. He fluffed up his back and motioned for me to get on. I couldn't believe I was about to get on a giant swan and fly to who-knows-where to meet the prince.

This all felt like a dream but I knew it wasn't so. I got on and we flew around and over the castle. It was wonderful. I felt so free, feeling the air on my face. I started to feel a little cold and the swan could tell, so he fluffed his feathers again to cover my arms from the cold wind.

We flew over a huge garden and in the center of the garden was a gazebo that was all lit up. In the middle of the huge gazebo stood Demitri, tall and sleek in a dark black and dark red velvet suit and a white ruffled shirt. Draped over him was a black velvet cape and he was wearing a black leather bat-like mask and white gloves to match his shirt.

I could see and feel his piercing eyes staring at me as the giant black swan descended from the sky and landed in front of the gazebo. The swan turned its head towards me. I scratch his head as if to say 'Thank you'.

Demitri came over to help me off the swan. "I see you've received my gifts. I hope you did not mind my friend here coming to get you and escort you to me."

"Of course not," I said as I looked around this fairytale of a gazebo. There were twinkling lights floating all around and what looked like iridescent roses and orchids so thin and shiny they almost looked like colored crystal.

In the center was a small table for two with a draped silk and lace tablecloth. On the table were fruit, seafood, steak that looked to be very rare, and pastry.

I looked back at the black swan one last time. "I never imagined flying on a swan. It made me feel exhilarated and free." As I petted the swan's head and neck, I said, "Thank you, Demitri."

"No, no, my dear sweet Murranda." He took my gloved hand in his and kissed the back of it. Even though he had on his gloves, I could still feel a coldness coming from his hands. When he kissed the back of my hand with his ice cold breath, a cold shiver came upon me. My legs got weak and I prayed I wouldn't fall or faint in front of him. I blushed and turned my head away from his piercing eyes. It seems that every time I am around him I blush and have a hard time looking into his eyes.

"I should be the one thanking you for honoring me by accepting my dinner invitation and allowing me to escort you to your first Ball. You look simply exquisite. You look so much like your mother, but, may I add, even more beautiful, if that is even possible." He then looked at the swan and smiled, "Thank you, old friend. You may go now."

As the swan flew away, Demitri twirled me around the gazebo and guided me to our table. Everything was so magical. He snapped his fingers and, as if by magic, the bottle of wine on our table poured itself into my glass.

"I can't believe you did all this for me," I said, trying to look into his eyes.

"Well," he replied, "when I heard this was going to be your very first Ball I knew I had to make it unforgettable, something you will remember forever."

"I know this will be a night I will always treasure." I exclaimed.

We sat and enjoyed the wonderful dinner and talked and laughed for what seemed like hours. He told me all about himself and his family and how far back his family had lived in the Shadow Lands.

Then he told me how his family came to meet Phoebe and Pheonna and how they took the two of them as their own, but without turning them into vampires. I wondered how someone with such kindness could also hold so much darkness and evil within himself.

Maybe everyone was wrong about the prince. Just because he might have come from generations of darkness and evil does not mean that he has to continue the cycle. Maybe he wants to break free from his family's ways.

Just then, we began to hear the wonderful music coming from inside the castle and emanating through the air. We both knew that the music meant this wonderful private dinner for two had to come to an end. Even though I was sad to see this special time end, I was very excited to see and finally be a part of this magical Masquerade Ball and all its wonders.

# Chapter 11

While I listened to the music, I looked across the table and smiled at Demitri, "I guess we should be heading to the party. I'm sure there are people looking for us. This dinner was wonderful. So far this evening has been more than I have ever dreamed. Thank you. I can't wait to see what else is in store for me."

"I plan to make this whole night exceed all of your dreams and expectations," Demitri replied as he walked around the table and gracefully took my hand.

We started to walk towards the castle. I was so excited to be going to my very first Ball. I wanted to get there as quickly as possible and, before I knew it, as if by magic, we were transported to the entrance of the Grand Ballroom. One minute I was with Demitri in his royal garden, and in a smoky flash, he and I were in the
Grand Ballroom. It was unbelievable.

When the horns blew to announce the guests' arrival, it startled me. I suddenly felt shy when I heard the guards announce, Prince Demitri and his lovely date, Lady Murranda Delarenzo, had arrived. I could feel all eyes gazing at us as we walked down the red-carpeted staircase. When they called out my name as his escort, I was sure that did not sit well with my father and friends.

Just then, high above a huge open window that was attached to a balcony over-looking the Ballroom there were two exquisite Pegasus. One was pure white, with Phoebe riding it, the other was a solid ebony black, which Pheonna rode. It was clear they truly loved making an entrance.

Once they arrived and everyone cheered, Demitri raised his arms to get everyone's attention. Feeling quite intimidated, I stood beside him, with everyone staring at us, and I waited with baited breath for the prince's welcoming announcement.

"Welcome, everyone. I truly hope you have been enjoying your stay here as we have been celebrating these two wonderful sisters during our annual, Weekend of Peace Celebration. I know you have been anxiously awaiting our grand Masquerade Ball. So, with no further ado, let the entertainment, the dancing, and other festivities begin."

The prince clapped his hands and fireworks illuminated the Ballroom sky. The entire Ballroom was decorated to perfection in draped silk and lace, with sparkling, crystal chandeliers floating in the air. Everyone was dressed in their finest costumes.

Even mermaids were in attendance. Pheonna and Phoebe made it possible for mermaids to walk on land, even though it was not a full moon cycle. The ones who wanted to keep their fins were able to magically float in the air. One could see bubbles coming from their gills, as if they were in some kind of clear water.

Even all the four-legged creatures were in costumes and masks, from the werewolves to the unicorns and Pegasus to my friend, Grey Sky. I even saw some dragons in costumes, as well.

I then began thinking of Jett, hoping that Phoenix was back here in the castle looking for him. I prayed she was alright.

At once, I was astonished to notice that the people in the portraits hung on the walls were in costume. How could that be? I swore the last time I saw those same portraits they were in different outfits. I had to remind myself that I was in an enchanted castle where anything was possible.

I looked to my right and saw a huge, golden cage with Cozmo the Golden Owl in costume and wearing what looked to be a thinly laced emerald and onyx mask. He was being hand-fed grapes and sitting so proudly, as if he were the fairest of us all. I had to laugh and shake my head.

Just then, I saw Glitz and Flutter running toward me, each the size of a small child and both wearing glittery fairy costumes with masks of feathers and leaves.

"WOW, Murranda," Flutter signed, "Glitz and I almost did not recognize you. You look amazing."

"Oh, thank you, Flutter," I signed back. "But look at the two of you. You both look wonderful."

Glitz looked at me with a shocked expression. "Murry, when did you learn to talk to Flutter?"

I didn't know how to respond to that, but I said, "Well I can't really explain how it happened but somehow, I can." Then I noticed his expression changed from shock to concern and worry.

"Your father and Jeffery have been looking for you. Would you like us to take you to them? I think I know where they are."

Glitz was about to grab my hand but Demitri grabbed both of my hands away from him. "You can go to your father after I have the first dance. Remember, Murranda dear, you did say I could have that." He looked at me with the sexiest smile I had ever seen. Glitz and Flutter were about to grab me away from him until I looked at them with a look that said, *Don't come any further you two*.

"Demitri is right Glitz. I told him he could have the first dance. I will go see Father, Jeffery and the rest of you afterwards. Have my father or Jeffery dance with Phoebe. I'm sure she would love that."

So the prince and I walked to the center of the dance floor. I could feel all eyes on us. I started to feel a little shy again.

Demitri asked, "What kind of dance would you like your first dance to be at your first Ball?"

I thought very hard for a bit, then said, "Mmm, well part of me would like a Viennese waltz, but then again maybe something more dark and powerful."

"Like a tango?" He asked.

"Yes."

"Well then," he added as he looked over at his orchestra. They were dressed in vampire costumes and masks. They started to play an eerie, yet romantic waltz.

The prince took my hand, and we began dancing across the dance floor. It was the most magical and romantic felling I have ever had. I felt as if I were floating on air. It was as though everyone in the Ballroom was no longer there and it was just the two of us. Throughout the dance we looked into each other's eyes. I felt as if he was looking into my soul. My whole body trembled. Demitri gave me a smirk, as if to let me know all was okay. Just then the music changed to something less then innocent. The music was now stronger and very passionate. Demitri pulled me in closer to him.

At that very moment someone yelled, "GET YOUR COLD HANDS OFF OF HER!"

I looked over and saw my father running towards us, about to rip the prince away from me. I quickly threw out my arms and yelled back, "STOP FATHER. NOW!"

At that instant, something happened that completely shocked me and everyone else in the Ballroom. When I threw out my arms to tell my father to stop, he suddenly could not move at all. The more he tried, the stiffer he became.

"Did I just do that?" I asked as I looked at my hands.

Demitri took his finger and placed it on my chin. He turned my face toward his and said, "I see you are finding out just what you can do. Breathe Murranda. Relax. He is okay. You wanted him to stop so he stopped. Now would you like to continue our dance or would you like to face your father?"

I looked at my father and then looked back at Demitri, who reassured me, "He is not hurt. The moment you are ready to talk to him he will be able to move again."

I looked at my father again and said, "I'm sorry Father, but as I told Glitz and Flutter, I promised the prince the first dance. When it is over, I will come find you and we can talk some more. I will even save you a dance or two as well."

I turned back to Demitri, "So, where were we?"

Demitri motioned to the orchestra to continue playing. The passionate music began again.

"Let's see if you can tango as good as your mother did," Demitri said with a smirk.

"I guess there is only one way to find out now, isn't there," I replied sarcastically.

Just like that, the prince and I began to tango.

# Chapter 12

Demitri pulled me closer and tighter for the tango. I could feel my heart racing and could hardly breathe. As closely as we were dancing, I thought I would feel his heart beating as well, but he is a vampire. Either he does not have a heart or, if he does, it beats so faintly I couldn't feel it.

His eyes were looking deeply into mine as we glided across the floor. The music and the dancing were so intense it seemed to become a competition to see who could tango best. With each step and each beat of the music the dance became more and more intense, so not another sound except the music and the stomping of our feet was heard.

I tried to look away from his staring eyes because I was not used to the feelings I was having. Part was excitement and another part was fear. There was even something else I had never felt before that I could not explain. I looked away and, when I did, I noticed Pheonna staring at me with a look of hatred and disgust. She seemed to be so irate at what she was seeing that her face was turning red and her hand was balling up into a fist. I did not understand why, so I tried to just ignore it.

Near the end of the tune, the prince lifted me up, twirled me around, and gently thrust me back to the ground, at the same time lifting my hands up towards him.

Before the tango ended, he quickly bent over so that his face was so close to mine our foreheads touched. I could feel his cold breath on me. Our faces were not even an inch apart. If we were to move our mouths, they would touch in a kiss, but we dared not.

Just then, he quickly pulled back and turned away from me as if something was wrong. I didn't know what to think or say. I knew my father was not happy about what he was seeing, and I'm sure our dance was making his blood boil.

As the tango ended and the next tune began, I noticed Demitri had vanished. I could not understand why. Did I do something wrong? Was it my father or my friends? Why did he leave so suddenly? As everyone in the Ballroom began to dance, I walked in the direction I had last seen him walking before he vanished. Then someone grabbed my arm and I smiled, thinking it was Demitri playing a trick on me. As soon as I turned around I saw it was my father.

"That's it! I've had it!" My father yelled as he pulled me way from the dance floor. "We are leaving now, Murranda! I knew you were not safe here. He is not going to do to you what he wanted to do to your mother all those years ago. We are going home and don't you dare tell me no!"

I quickly snatched my arm away from him and looked straight into his eyes. I planted my feet firmly on the floor and yelled back, "I'm NOT GOING ANYWHERE WITH YOU, FATHER!"

"Sunshine, you don't understand the magnitude of this situation," Father tried to explain. "This may be the Weekend of Peace, but as far as that blood-sucking prince is concerned, there is NO

PEACE. His obsession with the Prophesy is all there is. He will do to you what he wanted and tried to do to your mother, and with the last breath in my body I will NEVER let that happen. You can be mad at me all you want, but if doing so keeps you safe, then so be it."

As Father pulled on me and kept ranting and raving about my safety and this so called Prophesy, I noticed my friends coming toward me and wondering what was going on.

I could not take it anymore. I could not take his constant ranting about the prince and this Prophesy and my safety. I just held my hands up to my head.

I closed my eyes and shook my head back and forth repeating, "ENOUGH! ENOUGH! Father I just wish you and Jeffery would go home and leave me be. I wish you had never followed me here. Just go. Go home both of you, now."

I was so mad and tired. I wanted so badly to have him gone that when I finally opened my eyes I could not believe what I saw, or should I say what I didn't see. Father and Jeffery were both gone. All that was left in their places were the masks they had worn.

I looked around in a confused panic, not knowing what was really happening. I called out, "Father? Jeffery?" Hoping someone had an answer, I asked, "Where did they GO?"

Out of nowhere, Phoebe suddenly appeared. "Are you okay Murranda?" She placed her hand on my shoulder and turned me towards her. I kept looking around for my father and Jeffery. Phoebe said, "You need to calm down now, my dear. I saw what was going on between you and your father"

"Then please tell me what happened. One moment I was talking to my father and the next he and Jeffrey were gone. I was trying to get him to understand that this was MY journey, and I was tired of him trying to get me to leave and stop my journey."

I continued to explain, "He and my mother had their adventures and now it is my turn to have my own. I was trying to tell him that he cannot stop me, that I am going to see my journey through, even if that means staying in this castle for the celebration, but he refused to see things my way. I got so fed up with his ranting that I wished he and Jeffery had never followed me here. I wanted them to go back home on their own and let me have some peace. Then, just like that, they were both gone."

I pleaded, "So please, someone, anyone, tell me what just happened to Father and Jeffery."

Phoebe looked at my friends and said, "All of you, I need to talk to Murranda alone for a moment."

Turning to face him, Phoebe said, "In fact, Jett, I know you have been searching for your friend, Phoenix. Let me first assure you that she is fine and is still the same Phoenix you know. She has just evolved into who she really is. I saw her earlier with her birth mother. They are here in the castle. I told her to wait for you at the large balcony where my sister and I entered before the Ball began."

To the others she said, "So you go. We will meet back at the Ballroom."

When Jett heard his beloved Phoenix was back in the castle, his face just lit up. Jett, Nessa, Serena, Glitz, Flutter and Sky went to meet Phoenix. For some reason, Deena stayed behind. She looked down at Father's mask on the floor where he had been standing. I could have sworn I saw tears flowing from her eyes.

At that moment, Phoebe pulled me away and led me to the area of the Ballroom where there were chairs and tables. The castle servants were walking around asking if anyone wanted an appetizer or a drink. Phoebe and I sat at a small table in the corner.

Phoebe took two drinks off a serving tray. "Here, this should help," she said as she handed me a drink.

I took a long sip and then a deep breath. "Okay, I am fine now. I just need to know what happened back there." I grabbed her arms from across the table.

Phoebe took my hands into hers. "Remember what your father and I tried to explain to you about exactly who you are and where your mother and her family were from."

"Yes," I replied in confusion, "but what does that have to do with what happened to Jeffery and my father?"

"Think back, Murranda. Remember when we found you on the floor in your room? You told us one minute you were with the prince at the Ghostly Falls. You said you told him, at one point on your journey you died and came back. You said hearing about all that confused and frightened you so much that all you could think about was getting back to your room so you didn't have to hear any more about it?"

Phoebe continued, "You told your father and me, that just like that, you transported yourself back to your room, where we found you, thanks to your magical rose. We tried to explain how it was possible and why."

"Yes, of course I remember, but it's all so unbelievable I just can't fathom it. I mean how can a person be in one place and then, in the blink of an eye, be someplace far from there? None of this makes any sense. What does that have to do with Father and Jeffery? I did not disappear, they did."

Patiently, Phoebe explained, "Well, not only can you take yourself from one place to another in a blink, just by wanting it badly enough, you can also send others away."

I nodded, and she continued, "So when you got fed up with your father and the way he was acting, you sent him and Jeffery back home the moment you said you wished they had never followed you here and they should just go home themselves. Your powers are getting stronger."

It was still all so confusing to me. I didn't know what to think about all of it. "Does that mean they are back home?" I asked.

"Yes, and most likely in your garden looking at your rose," she said.

"Father is going to be even madder at me now."

"Well, not really my dear. When you sent them back home, you said you wished they had never even followed you here. So once they arrived home, it seemed to them they had never left, nor had they been here looking for you. It was as if time went backwards."

Phoebe explained, "In time, they will have a feeling of déjà vu. Rudy will realize what has happened because your mother did that to him many times in the past."

I looked at her, then looked back at the dance floor. I thought about all that had happened and wondered where Demitri was. The look on his face, when he turned away and left me in the middle of the dance floor, worried me.

I mean, this was my very first Ball, something I have dreamed of since I was a little girl. Now, here I am, but all I can think about is looking for Demitri and asking why he just left like he did. Everyone around me has been warning me to stay away from the Dark Prince, but I did not see what they saw.

I looked back at Phoebe as she continued to hold my hands. "I know what you are thinking right now," she said with a concerned tone in her voice.

I gave her a look as if to say, stop getting in my head, but I said, "If you know what I'm thinking, and if what you say is true about my father, and he is back home in the garden looking at the rose, that will only mean we both know what is going to happen next."

I speculated, "If I do what I am wanting to do, and Father can see what I do through the rose, then we know he will be coming back here. By then the Weekend of Peace will be over."

I looked at Phoebe and continued, "I know a part of you wants to help him get back here, for his own safety, before this is over, but Phoebe, as my friend, I beg you to leave this alone. The celebration will be over soon and, come sunrise, everyone will be leaving the castle and the Shadow Land. I will then continue on with my journey, away from here to who knows where. I am sure Father can follow me then."

"Fine," She said exhaustedly. "I will not help him find you as long as you are not in danger. You have my word. But if you are in any kind of danger, then I will use my abilities to get him to you."

"So be it!" I said. "Until then, this is my journey and my adventure. He has had his. All I ask is that everyone let me have mine. Now that I know what has happened to my father and Jeffery, and that they are okay, I need to find out if someone else is alright."

"Murry, the prince is fine," Phoebe said trying to get me to stay with her.

"I need to find out for myself. If nothing else, I deserve to know why he just left me in the middle of the dance floor like he did. That was embarrassing."

I rose from the table and leaned over to kiss Phoebe on the cheek and say, "Thanks for making me understand what happened to my father and calming me down a bit. I'll be okay, but I need to do this."

"Please understand. Remember, I am still wearing your necklace, even though it does not go with my gown." I snickered.

Phoebe looked at the necklace then looked at me. I was praying she could not tell it was not the same stone in the necklace.

She had given me the necklace so that it would warn me of danger. Shortly after my arrival at the Dark Castle, the prince and I were on a walk along the lake. As the prince got closer to me, the necklace began to vibrate and shine brightly as a warning of danger. I didn't recognize the prince as a threat, so when Demitri suggested I let him replace the stone so I could stay and enjoy the festivities at the castle without worrying about what the necklace would do, I agreed.

He replaced the stone and gave me the original one to save. He promised to restore it when I was ready to leave and continue my journey.

Phoebe did not seem to notice the difference in the necklace. She just smiled and let go of my hand.

I turned toward the dance floor and walked across it, looking around and hoping I would see the prince, but no luck. I headed away from the Ball and toward the hallways, thinking maybe he had returned to his chambers.

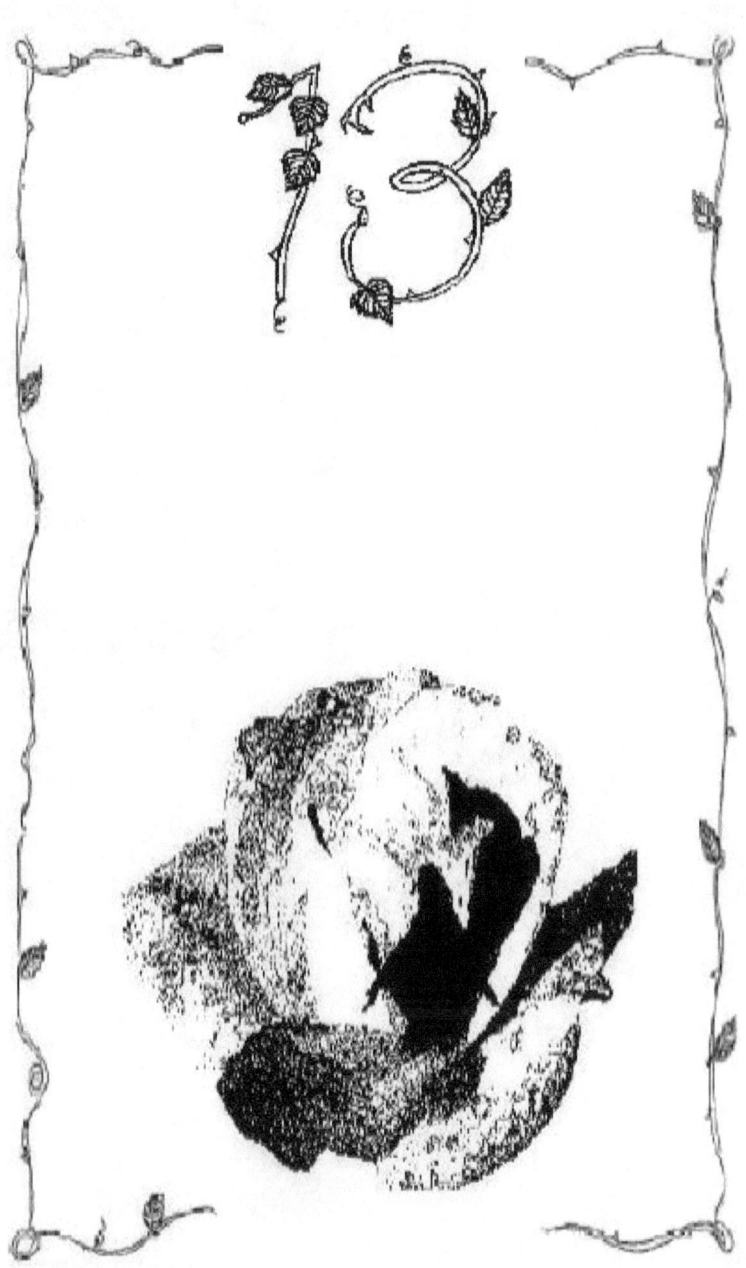

# Chapter 13

Meanwhile, in another part of the castle there was a hidden room where the Dark Sorceress, Pheonna, was pacing back and forth in anger, stomping her staff on the floor.

"How dare that little brat try to seduce my prince? Everyone thinks she is so innocent and sweet. If I don't put my plan into action soon, I will never become queen and rule beside my dear sweet prince."

Pheonna snapped her fingers to summon the pirate, Captain Darrell Blackheart. Instantly, in a purple cloud of smoke, Captain Darrell appeared with his back to her. His eyes were closed and he was leaning forward swaying back and forth as if he was drunk, which from his odor, he apparently was.

He kept leaning in further and further. "Arrgh, kiss me, my little red-headed beauty."

His speech was mumbled and slurred. He was about to lean in so far that he was going to fall on his face. With the help of Pheonna's magic fingers, he quickly turned around to face her. He continued leaning in until Pheonna put her hand up to stop his face from getting any closer. She then pushed him back to his feet.

"As tempting as that is, my Captain, I am not red-headed, so you must have been flirting with some other maiden. But that is beside the point. You and I have a lot to discuss."

She turned away and waved her hand in front of her nose to get rid of his odor from rum and filthy sweat.

Captain Darrell opened his eyes, looked around and saw that he was not where he thought he was. Once he saw Pheonna, he grinned that sexy grin of his. Then he grew serious, knowing if he didn't, he wouldn't get any more of those precious gold and golden weapons she promised him and his crew. Just thinking about all that gold was making his musky bearded mouth watery.

He asked, twisting his beard with his dirty fingers, "Arrg, my evil beauty, how do ye want this to go down?"

Pheonna looked at him with a sinister stare. "All you need to know right now is, once we leave here, you go to the location I showed you and you and your crew wait for my signal. I don't care how long it takes; you must wait there for my signal."

"Arrg, and what signal, pray tell, will I be waiting for?"

Pheonna just looked at him with frustration as she continued to explain her plan, "Once I send down the little brat, I mean Murranda, you and your crew of idiots take her and tie her up. Put her on your ship, then set sail far away from Xenophile."

"And head to Dragon Island were our treasure will be waiting for us," added the captain.

"Of course," she said with a seductive look. "Your precious treasure will be waiting for you at the center of Dragon Island, as long as you carry out my plan to the end. If I find out you did not do what we agreed on, there will be no treasure. Trust me. I will know if you have her."

Pheonna showed the captain the white rose so he could see that the shadow in the rose was of Murranda.

The captain looked closely at the rose and saw that it showed a shadow of Murranda looking for the prince. He quickly cleared his throat and said, "Arrg, don't you worry yer purty lil head Dearie. Me crew and I will be more than willing to take care of yer purty little problem. Once we take her to Dragon Island, then what do you want us to do with her?"

"I don't care what you do with that meddling little brat. You can toss her off your ship and feed her to the sharks. You can throw her in the dragons' cave and let them have her. Or, you can make her part of your crew. She is looking for adventure. I don't care what it is, as long as she stays far away from the prince."

Pheonna explained, "Captain, listen to me closely. After the guests enjoy their dancing, there will be entertainment presented by my sister and me. We will be doing a competition in magic. At the end of it I will ask Lady Murranda for her assistance in some magic tricks, one of them being I will make her disappear and then I will take her place."

The captain was a little puzzled when she said she would take Murranda's place. "So does that mean we are abducting you? If that is so, me dear, I have some rope right here, "he said as he held up some rope and was about to tie her up.

"No, you idiot! When I send her down to you, I will then change myself to appear as Murranda. Everyone will see she is fine and they will just think I made my normal grand exit from the party. All they will see is her, and you and your crew will take the real Murranda on your ship far away from Xeenoephillia. That is if you want all your precious gold."

She took hold of his dirty shirt and pulled tight, twisting it till it almost choked him.

The captain placed his hand on hers so she would let go. He assured her all would be done as she asked. Then they went over her plan again.

# Chapter 14

While the dark sorceress and the rugged captain continued to go over their scheme on how to get rid of the Lady Murranda, Jett, Nessa, Sky, Glitz, Flutter, and Serena ran to the huge balcony of the Ballroom, hoping to find their friend Phoenix. They were concerned for her safety, and more importantly, whether or not she was still the same Phoenix they knew. They were worried that somehow her transformation had changed her, not just physically but in every way. Jett ran around the balcony in a panic, calling out for her and searching everywhere.

"Brother, look up!" Nessa shouted as she tapped him on the shoulder to get his attention.

Jett looked up and saw Phoenix and three other dragons flying around in the sky. They were flying up and over each other having a grand time.

Jett could hear them laughing. The red

dragon looked down to where Jett and the others stood and said, "Look, sister dear, we have an audience. Can I give them a little scare?"

At that point Phoenix looked down to see what he was talking about and it was then she saw her beloved elf and her other friends shouting and pointing, trying to get her attention.

"Don't you dare, Drake!" Phoenix yelled. She quickly flew in front of him to stop him from doing whatever he was going to do. "Those are my friends!"

"Oh really?" The white dragon interrupted. "So that must mean the young handsome elf calling your name down there is the same young elf that has stolen my daughter's heart. I must meet him."

The four of them flew down and transformed into their human and elflike selves.

Phoenix was so excited to see Jett that as soon as she transformed back into her old self she ran up and hugged him tightly, not noticing his shocked expression until she finally let go and looked into his eyes. She looked at the rest of her friends and noticed their expressions, as well.

"Jett, its okay. It's me, Phoenix. I'm still the same girl. Please tell me you believe," she pleaded as she held his face in her hands.

He shook his head and looked deep into her eyes. There he saw his beloved Phoenix and he hugged her tightly.

"What happened to you after the competition?" He asked with concern in his voice. "We were all worried and I looked all over the Shadow Land for you. Where did you run off to?"

"Don't you mean flew off to?" Nessa said as she ran up and hugged Phoenix from behind. "Who knew you were such a hot head." The three of them burst into laughter.

Phoenix explained, "When I transformed into my dragon state for the first time, I didn't know what to think or do. When I saw everyone's reaction, especially yours, I could not take it. I wanted to just run and hide and that was when I saw Rayne and Drake in their dragon forms. Something inside told me to follow them and they would have the answers to what had happen to me. So, I did."

"They took me to Dragon Island," Phoenix continued, "and can I just say, that once I calmed down and just followed them, I started to feel as if this was the real me. I felt as free as a dragon. When we arrived at Dragon Island I found out it was my true home."

"I am from royal blood and I was taken away from the island and my family for my own protection. Then I was reunited with my true mother," She explained to everyone as she pointed to Rayn, Drake, and her mother.

"Jett, this is my mother, Queen Phazha."

"So, you are the young elf that stole my daughter's heart," Queen Phazha said as she approached Phoenix, Jett, and the others. "You must be Nessa his sister and you two must be Glitz and Flutter, and you my furry friend must be Grey Sky. Phoenix has told us so much about you all on our journey here. I was hoping to also see my old gypsy friend, Phoebe. I wanted to personally thank her for saving my daughter's life."

"The last we saw of her was in the Ballroom near the dance floor with Murranda," said Glitz. "We can take you to her if you like Your Majesty."

"That would be wonderful," she said.

They were all about to go find Phoebe when, out of nowhere, Phoebe appeared.

"Did I hear my name called?" Phoebe giggled. "Your Highness, it gives me such joy to see you again. I am so sorry to hear about your husband, but I see you have finally been reunited with your beloved daughter."

Addressing her, Phoebe said, "Phoenix, I am so glad you found your mother. Now you will be able to have all your questions answered. But first, please join the rest of the guests in the Grand Ballroom for our Masquerade Ball. Our entertainment will be starting soon."

Queen Phazha walked up and gave Phoebe a big hug with tears of joy in her eyes. "I can never thank you enough for saving my daughter and raising her all these years."

"It has been my pleasure, Your Highness. I have always had much love and respect for you, your family and people. Your daughter has grown up to be the best of both you and your husband. She has your fiery spirit and curiosity, plus your husband's determination and some of his stubbornness," Phoebe said as they all laughed.

"But Phoebe, we are not dressed for the Ball." Phoenix said, as she looked at herself and then looked at Jett, Nessa and Serena and the wonderful costumes they were wearing.

"We can fix that," said Rayne. She looked around for some type of fountain or lake and spotted a fountain in the middle of a nearby garden under the balcony. She jumped upon the edge of the balcony and dove down. Everyone rushed to the edge to see what in the world she was doing.

The moment Rayne's fingers touched the cold water spewing out of the fountain, she flew back up into the air with a stream of water behind her and following her up higher and higher in the air. While she was still in her elf-like form, she spiraled up and down and across the air with the water copying her every movement. She started to slow down and, as she did, the dark and light blue of the water began forming what looked like splash designs on her clothes. When the water splashed on her face it formed a bluish mask. She looked amazing as she came back down to join everyone.

Then Drake gave his devilish smile and jumped high into the air, transforming into his dragon form. He found a small pile of rocks, and with one stroke of his massive wings, he blew them into the air. He then blew fire at them and made them melt into magma. Then, just as Rayne had done with the water, Drake spiraled in the air with the magma copying his movements.

They could see it forming patterns on his scaly skin. When Drake changed back to his human form the magma kept some of the scaly pattern on his skin and mask. Everyone was very impressed.

Phoebe looked at Phoenix and her mother, saying, "Your Highness, it would be my honor if you would allow me to create your costume." She took Queen Phazha by the hand and guided her to a nearby diamond-covered chandelier. With a flick of her finger, Phoebe made the chandelier drop on the Queen. Not quite knowing what Phoebe was doing the Queen's guard, Rayne, quickly grew her dragon tail out and whipped it out to grab Phoebe by the neck and restrain her.

Phoenix shouted, "Rayne, WAIT. Look!" Just then the chandelier floated back up and there stood the Dragon Queen in a diamond jeweled gown and mask with specks of diamond in her long silver hair.

Everyone was speechless. Phoenix looked around at all her friends and was amazed by how they all looked in their costumes. But then she looked at what she was wearing and started to wonder what she was going to do. Phazha could see the worried look in her daughter's eyes.

She picked up two nearby candles and walked with them to her daughter. "Oh my dear Phoenix. Let me guess. You are wondering if you can do what you just saw Rayne and Drake do. You have the same abilities my dear." She handed her the two candles. "First, think about how you want your costume and mask to look, and how you want it to fit. Now close your eyes and picture it in your mind. Do you see it?"

Phoenix closed her eyes and could see her costume is such detail. She excitedly nodded her head.

"Now gently blow on the candles without blowing them out. You are going to form a firewall with the candles."

"I can form the firewall for you, Phoenix." Nessa jumped in to help. "My teacher has been helping me with my new-found gift. Can I help?"

Phoenix nodded, so Nessa looked at the two flickering candles and with her hands she commanded the flames to rise up bigger and wider to form a fiery wall. Then Phazha stood behind

Phoenix and nudged her to walk up to the flames. The flames touched her skin as she slowly walked up to and through it. She then started to spin around and around, and as she did the flames followed her movements and started to form her costume and mask. Once Phoenix stopped spinning the fiery wall disappeared and the candles went out. What stood in front of everyone was Phoenix in a fiery costume with flames of different shades of reds, oranges, yellows, and golds. Her mask was of flames all around her eyes.

"I DID IT!" She screamed. "I just thought really hard about the costume I wanted to wear, and I DID IT."

"And I've never seen you look more beautiful," Jett said, taking her by the arm and twirling her around. "Now that you are here and ready for the Ball, can we join the rest of the guests, and may I have the first dance with you?"

Phoenix blushed and nodded. So Jett, Phoenix, her mother and the rest of them went back

to the Grand Ballroom to enjoy the Masquerade
Ball.

# Chapter 15

While Phoenix, Jett, Queen Phazha, and the others went back to the Ballroom, I continued searching for Demitri.

Why did he dance with me and just leave me in the middle of the dance floor like he did with no word? It just didn't make sense. Was it because of the way my father reacted when he saw us dancing together? With each turn I kept hitting dead ends, no prince.

"I wish there was some way I could find you Demitri," I said out loud. "Where are you?"

Just then, the garnet ring I was wearing started to glow. Phoebe had given the ring to me when she gave me the necklace. I looked more closely at the ring, to see why it was glowing. In the center of the stone in the ring, I could see something moving. I looked harder into it. It was Demitri. He was pacing back and forth inside what looked to be his chambers.

I said, "Alright, ring, you showed me where he is. Can you now show me how to get there?"

Just then I felt the ring pulling my hand to the right as if to tell me to turn right down the hallway. So I did. Then I felt it pulling me forward then to the left then forward again down a long dark hallway, so dark that the only light in the hallway was from my ring. I kept walking till I reached a tall, dark, burgundy double door with gold markings and a golden handle.

I was about to knock on the door when I heard voices coming from inside. One was Demitri's voice and the other seemed to be a woman's voice. From what I could hear, it seemed to be an intense conversation, and by what I could tell, it had something to do with me.

I decided to let myself in by knocking on the door as I opened it. I entered the room and thought I saw, but wasn't quite sure, a woman who looked like a floating ghost talking to Demitri. But when I shook my head in disbelief the woman appeared more like Demitri, a vampire. So I just brushed it off, as if my eyes were playing tricks on me.

"Excuse me. I hope I'm not interrupting anything," I said as I entered the room. "I became very concerned after our dance, when you just left me in the middle of the dance floor without a word."

"I am so sorry, Murranda. Please forgive me." Demitri replied, stumbling over his words. "I just …I just needed to…"

"What my dear sweet son is trying to say is, he was needed up here during the time of your dance. I was calling for him in a way that only he could hear," the woman said as she came to me and introduced herself. "I am Natasha, Demitri's mother and Queen, well I prefer Mother, of the Shadow Land. Oh Son you told me she looked like her dear sweet mother, but I believe this flower is even more exquisite."

All I could do was blush. "Thank you." I said as I tried to bow to her without stumbling over my dress. For some reason I was very nervous. "May I say it is a pleasure to meet you, Your

Highness? I understand now. I was just concerned. I assumed since I had not seen you throughout the celebration that… ahh that…."

"Let me guess. You thought I, too, was no longer among the living, just as your beloved mother, Morinda."

"Well yes, I suppose, as much as a vampire can be among the living. But wait, you also knew my mother?"

"Yes, I did," she smiled. "Your mother and I crossed paths many times in the past. The reason you have not seen me in any of the celebrations is, even though I am not dead, I am also not truly alive. I am a trapped spirit. You might say I am in limbo. I can only go as far as my portrait goes," she explained as she pointed to a portrait frame that was on the wall and had an outline of her.

She asked, "Have you not noticed how the portraits around the castle now have on masquerade costumes where they didn't before the Ball began? We are called living portraits. We can go in and out of the frames, but we can only go so far. We can also live forever as long as the portraits themselves do not break or get burned."

I was still not sure what she meant by all that but I nodded anyway.

"Now Son," she said as she turned and reached out for Demitri's hand to pull him closer to me, "I thank you for helping me earlier, but I have kept you away from this sweet girl long enough. Now you two go back to the Ball. I'm sure everyone is wondering where the prince has gone. You don't want to miss the entertainment."

As a separate thought, she said, "Oh, and by the way, Murranda dear, I hope after this Weekend of Peace celebration is over and everyone leaves our fair home you will consider staying on a while longer, at least until the Blood Moon rises. It is such a wonderful site to see as it reflects off the water near the Ghostly Falls. Please tell me you will stay for that. I promise nothing will happen to you as long as you are with my son. Isn't that right Son?"

Demitri just looked at his mother very sternly, then leaned in and kissed her cheek. "We must be going now Mother. We will discuss that later, but now we will get back to the Ball."

We left his room while his mother stood there watching us with an intense look in her eyes.

"Is everything alright, Demitri? You have been acting strangely ever since our dance."

"Of course, everything is fine. Let's just get back to the Ball. I'm sure your friends are wondering what happened to you, and I can just imagine how your father is doing right about now," he smirked, quickly trying to change the subject.

With everything that was going on with Demitri and his mother, I almost forgot about Father and what I did to him and Jeffery. Demitri was not aware of what had happened. "I don't think we have to worry about Father for a while," I said.

He stopped and looked at me, surprised, "What is that supposed to mean? When I last saw him I could tell he wanted to strike me dead."

"I grew so tired of how my father was acting that I wished him and Jeffery home. So they are back home on the mainland, in the garden my father and I built together. I'm sure he's sitting there looking at my rose as if they had never left," I replied guiltily.

"You did what?" he gasped. "I guess you are coming into your powers quicker then we all anticipated." He grabbed my hand and we walked into the Grand Ballroom.

"Now we can enjoy the rest of the festivities in peace," I said, as we smiled at each other. Then he twirled me back onto the center of the dance floor for another dance.

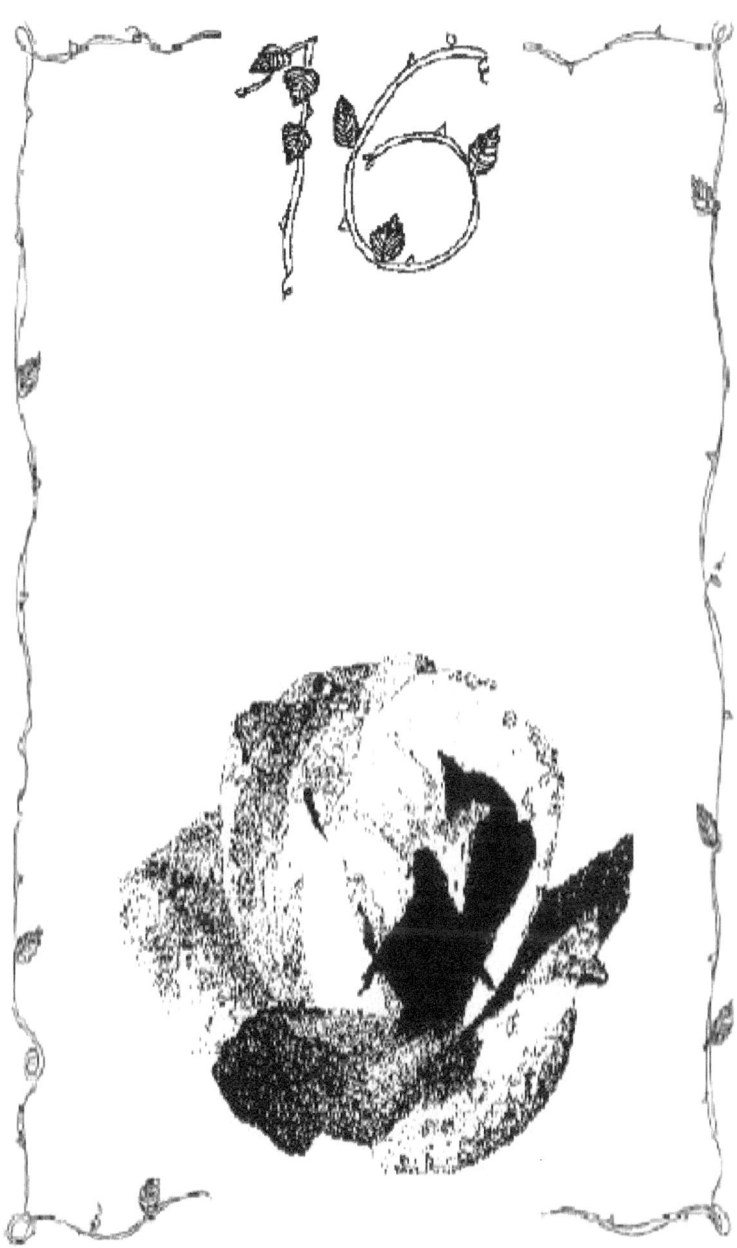

# Chapter 16

As the night went on, everyone in the Dark Castle was enjoying the Ball. High above the crowd a huge golden cage was descending down into the center of the Ballroom. In the cage dressed in all his glittery wonder was Cozmo the Golden Owl. Even though he was frightened, knowing he was about to get handed off as a trophy to someone, he still fluffed his feathers in pride and strutted around his cage, waving at everyone as if he was the king and we were all his worshiping subjects.

It was time for the prince to announce the winner of the Grand Tournament that had occurred earlier in the day. As Cozmo made his entrance from above, Demitri kissed my hand and whispered in my ear, "In case you were wondering, I have not forgotten my earlier promise about your feathered friend."

I looked up at him and smiled because I knew Cozmo was going to be alright and not handed off to someone who would hurt him.

Then the prince walked over to the center of the Ballroom where Cozmo was. He raised his hands to calm the crowd, then said, "First, I again want to thank everyone who came and participated in the festival and competitions this weekend."

Bowing respectfully, Demitri announced, "I also want to thank the Royal Family of Xeenoephilia, King Fredrick, and his beautiful Queen Katherine, for participating in the festival as well."

"I'm sure everyone is anxious to learn who the grand winner of the tournament is, and will be the proud owner of their very own golden owl."

"Hold your tongue now. I am not a prize to be given away!" Cozmo fussed. "You can't capture someone like me and try to use me as some kind of trophy to be won! Some Weekend of Peace this is. Just wait; whenever I turn human again I am going to remember each and every one of you."

Phoebe, who was standing on the other side of the owl's cage with her sister, Pheonna, glared at Cozmo, and with a flick of her finger took away his voice. He kept flapping his beak but not a word was heard from him.

"Well done, sister," Pheonna said with a smirk as she winked at her sister. "I knew you still had a little evil in you."

"I wouldn't call it evil so much as maybe doing everyone a favor," she replied.

Demitri looked at the sisters and smiled as he tried to hold back his laughter. He then cleared his thoughts and resumed, "After adding up all the scores from the competitions, the winner of this year's event goes to Jett from Elfinia," Demitri announced.

I looked around for my beloved friend with pride and excitement. I was so relieved it was one of my friends who had won Cozmo. Now I knew he was safe for the time being. But just how safe I could not tell with a room full of pirates, rebels, greedy dwarfs and trolls all around.

Just then I saw Jett walking to the center of the Ballroom with Phoenix by his side. They both looked amazing, but I noticed something different about Phoenix. I couldn't quite put my finger on it.

I decided to just run down to congratulate Jett and see what he was going to do with the owl. I also wanted to get closer and see if I could figure out what was so different about Phoenix.

I called out to them as I got closer. "Jett! You won! That is great!" I gave both of them a hug and said, "Phoenix, last I heard, you somehow turned yourself into some massive phoenix dragon and flew far away from the castle. Where did you go? Is everything okay?"

"Yes, Murry, I am fine. When I transformed into my dragon form for the first time I didn't understand what was happening, and I needed answers. That is when I met Rayne and Drake, and they took me to a place called Dragon Island, outside of our land, where I could find my answers. That is where I was reunited with my mother, Queen Phazha, Queen of Dragon Island," Phoenix explained.

"WAIT! Mother? Queen? Then that would make you a princess," I laughed.

"What is so funny?" She asked.

"I'm sorry, Phoenix. I don't mean to be rude. I am happy that you found your real mother. But, you, a princess? The same young girl I met back at Elfinia, who handed me that note from Phoebe, could not be the same one I am seeing in front of me now. I would never have imagined you had come from royalty."

"What is that supposed to mean?" Drake abruptly interrupted and stood between Phoenix and me. "How dare you talk to Her Highness in that way, as if she were some commoner."

"At ease, Drake. That will be quite enough!" Queen Phazah said. "Remember, neither Phoenix nor her friends ever knew who she really was and where she had come from."

She tried to explain to Drake that I was not trying to be rude. For some reason the Queen kept staring at me as she talked.

She said, "So you are the Murranda everyone around here has been talking about. Please excuse me for staring but it is uncanny how much you look like your mother. I also heard that you created a unique flower. I would love to see it. Where are my manners? You would think that as a Queen I would first introduce myself instead of just carrying on a conversation."

"I am Phazha, Queen of Dragon Island. Your mother, Morinda, and I were very close friends. Is there anyway I can see this magical rose I have heard so much about?"

I looked around at everyone and asked, "Does anyone have one of my roses close by?"

Phoebe looked at me, "Murry remember you and the rose are one. So if you have any of your seeds left or need a rose, you can call upon it. For example, think about the rose you gave me. Now hold out your hand and call on it. Your father and I told you the truth about yourself and about some of your abilities, so you have the ability to call on it."

"You can do it, Murry. Remember when you were in Elfinia and you called upon the necklace?" Glitz reminded me.

So I held out my hand and thought very hard about the Murry Rose I had given to Phoebe. Before I knew it, I was holding it in my hand. The single white rose that held the shadow of me was in a small, gem-encrusted flower pot.

Phazha looked at the flower intensely. She saw a shadow of me holding the rose and also saw herself moving around looking at the rose.

"This is astonishing! I have never in my life seen anything like this before. You are telling me that whoever has this rose, the Murry Rose, can see you and where you go at anytime and as well as who you meet along the way? "Simply astonishing."

"Will you still be continuing your journey after the celebration here is over?" I nodded, yes. "Then I must have one of your roses. I would love to watch you on your journey, and I promise if I see you in any kind of danger I will send out my dragon army to help you. You and your friends have let my daughter join you on this quest, and you all have watched over her. Now I would like to have a rose so I can watch over you."

"Your Majesty, you can have my rose," Phoebe said as she took the rose out of my hands and handed it to Phazha. "In fact, here, let me send it to your palace." She waved her hands and made the rose disappear. "Now the rose is safe on Dragon Island in your chambers."

"Thank you, my friend," said Phazha.

Cozmo the owl kept patting his foot on his cage louder and louder trying to get our attention as he watched us talking. "Hum, hum. If you lads and lassies don't mind, can you get me out of here?" He yelled.

"Oh, be quiet you overgrown chicken," Deena said as she walked up from behind him to join the rest of us.

"I am an OWL, and this overgrown, pointy-eared idiot has somehow won me. If he knows what's good for him, he will set me free."

We all laughed as I opened his cage to grab him out and set him on Jett's shoulder.

Cozmo was about to fly off. "I wouldn't leave if I were you," I said to him. "There are too many pirates and others who would just love to get their hands on you and your golden feathers."

Cozmo hugged Jett's neck tightly with his wings. "You'd better protect me with your life, my pointy-eared friend. I am a valuable commodity." Everyone had to laugh.

Prince Demitri came to congratulate Jett for his win and then asked for everyone's attention. "Ladies and Gentlemen, please take a seat. We are about to have our final entertainment. Our special guests of honor, Phoebe and Pheonna, will astonish us and delight us all with their spells, magic and illusions. It is truly something to see."

All those who had been a part of the weekend celebrations in the past knew exactly what the prince was talking about. You could see how excited everyone was getting. So my friends and I took our seats to await this performance.

# Chapter 17

Everyone took a seat in order to watch the entertainment. The sisters were flying high above the castle walls on the Pegasus given to them by the prince.

"Another year of celebrating our reunion has come and about to be gone and I still have not convinced you to stay home with me," Pheonna said to her sister. "This will always be your home. The Shadow Land welcomed us as family when our own family left us, Sister Dear. Why must you feel so loyal to those on the mainland?"

"I can ask you the same thing. The Shadow Land represents all that is evil and corrupt, everything I stand against. You are right Sister, they did raise us as their own. Without them there is no telling if we would still be here today. For that I will always be grateful to them. But who they are and the things they do, I can't condone. I know you feel close to them. That is the reason I have not tried to stop them," Phoebe said putting her hands on her sister's cheeks. "My love for you, Sister, is the only reason I still come here. If not for that, I would never set one foot here again."

"Now that your new friend, Murranda, is finding out what, I mean, who she really is and what she is capable of, are you afraid that the Prophesy will come true and this might truly be the end of your beloved home? It does seem as if she and the prince are getting closer by the minute."

"I stopped Demitri before when it came to Murranda's mother, Morinda. I will stop him again," Phoebe assured her.

"Don't be foolish, Sister. It will happen and I will be front and center when it all takes place, even though I should be by our prince's side as his queen."

Then Pheonna blocked her thoughts from her sister. *If all goes as planned, I will be.* She then telepathically told the pirate, Captain Darrell, to get ready and to also have his ship and crew ready to set sail.

"Phoebe looked puzzled at her sister as she noticed Pheonna had a devilish smile on her face.

"Is everything okay, Sister? For some reason I cannot seem to tell what you are thinking right now."

"Phoebe dear, of course all is okay. I am just thinking about the performance we are about to do. I have some new tricks up my sleeves this year that will surprise everyone, even you."

"Well then, let's not keep our guests waiting any longer."

"After you, Sister Dear," Pheonna said as she let her sister go ahead of her.

They flew towards the castle wall and with a point of their fingers they created a large, round window portal, then flew through it and into the castle above the Grand Ballroom. Once they flew in, the portal closed. Everyone in the Ballroom cheered as the sisters made their grand entrance. As they flew around us they pointed in different directions and made immense rings of fire.

The Pegasus would fly through the rings even though some appeared to be too small for them to fly through. When they approached those small rings of fire, the sisters and the Pegasus would shrink down to fit through them. Once they reached the other side they returned to their normal sizes. The crowd cheered.

Then the two sisters were on each side of the room facing each other and the drums started to beat faster and faster. The sisters started to race towards each other at such a speed the crowd was frightened at what might happen next. When it looked like a crash was about to occur, the two Pegasus burst into a fireworks display and the sisters descended into the center of the Ballroom.

Everyone, including the Kings and Queens of the different lands and Prince Demitri himself stood up and cheered.

"Ladies and Gentlemen, my sister and I want to thank you all for coming," Phoebe announced to the crowd.

"It has been wonderful seeing some familiar faces again and meeting new ones," Pheonna chimed in. "We have truly enjoyed seeing a lot of the competitions this year. At this time, my sister and I would love to have our turn, as we entertain you with magic and spells and even some illusions."

"So, without further ado, let the magic begin," the sisters said simultaneously.

Phoebe began the show. She noticed a tribe of Centaurs with a smaller, unique Centaur sitting with them. Normally, Centaurs are half human and half horse; however, this one was half girl and half lamb. She belonged to the Stallion clan.

Jereshane and his wife Tegan found this orphan child lamb and raised her as one of their own. Her name was MaryLamb. Even though she is half lamb instead of half horse like most Centaurs, in her mind and heart, she is a true Centaur. If anyone were to call her a lamb, she would stomp on their foot as hard as she could.

MaryLamb was holding her doll while watching all the magic the sisters were presenting onstage. Phoebe walked to the child and whispered in her ear. Then MaryLamb stood and walked with Phoebe to the center of the Ballroom.

Phoebe asked if she could hold her doll for a bit. She held the doll up so the crowd could see it. Then she let go of the doll, and it just floated in midair. She began circling one hand above the doll's head and the other below its feet. She moved her hands wider and wider apart, making the little doll grow until it became the same size as MaryLamb. The child was so excited she started jumping up and down.

Phoebe then made the doll do tumbles and flips around little MaryLamb. The little girl could not believe what she was seeing. The crowd cheered. MaryLamb went to hug her doll and to her astonishment, the doll actually hugged her back. It was so sweet to watch. Then the doll quickly shrank down to her normal size, and MaryLamb didn't know what to do or think. You could tell that part of her was sad.

"Well, if you think that was special, MaryLamb," Pheonna said as she took MaryLamb by the hand and pulled her away from her sister Phoebe and toward her, "have you ever dreamed of flying?"

"All the time," MaryLamb said with excitement in her voice.

"Well, how would you like to do just that and fly back to your parents instead of walking all the way back there?"

MaryLamb was so excited all she could do was jump up and down with glee.

"All you have to do is flap your arms up and down like this," she said as she showed her how. So MaryLamb did just that and as she flapped her arms colorful feathers started to appear all over her arms and hands, so many brightly colored feathers pink, purple, blue, yellow and green. The more she flapped the more colors appeared to the point where she started to take flight.

With Pheonna's guidance, MaryLamb flew all around the Ballroom then Pheonna pointed to her and then pointed to the empty chair that was next to Tegan, MaryLamb's mother. She felt compelled to fly there but not until she had done a few flips in the air, and then she sat down by her mother. As soon as she sat down the bright, colorful feathers disappeared. Everyone was aghast. We all stood and cheered.

While the sisters continued to entertain us with all their magic and illusions, I looked over at little MaryLamb. She was flapping her arms trying to fly again. Then she grabbed her doll and threw it in the air trying to get it to grow again. To her disappointment, nothing happened.

The sisters kept dazzling us with amazing illusions such as Pheonna taking fire and shaping it into the form of a shark and chasing one of the mermaids around till the mermaid got fed up with it and with a flap of her tail and a little of her own magic, took the water from a nearby fountain and splashed the fiery shark till it vanished.

Then Phoebe walked up to some Lycons, one being a werewolf and the other a werecat, and by touching her hand on their heads she lifted their heads off their bodies and put the werewolf's head on the werecat's body then put the werecat's head on the werewolf's body. The two Lycons were so dumbfounded they did not know how to react. But before there was any kind of uproar between the two, Phoebe took one of her long silk scarves off her dress and placed it over both of their heads then quickly pulled it away, and the two Lycons were back to normal. Everyone except the Lycons cheered. They just looked at each other with disgust.

This went on until Pheonna noticed how the prince and I kept looking and grinning at each other. He was sitting on his thrown next to the other royal families, and I was sitting with my friends. Seeing us act this way did not sit well with Pheonna.

*"It's time. You and your crew better be ready and you better not fail me or else,"* she told Captain Darrell telepathically. He was waiting in a secret room right under the Ballroom floor.

Just then Pheonna jumped up into the air and started spinning around and around causing sparks to fly everywhere. She was spinning so fast she looked like a whirlwind. Everyone stood back, including her sister.

Once she knew she had everyone's attention, she slowed down. "Now that I have your attention," she said as she descended to the middle of the dance floor. "Normally my sister and I would do the last illusion together, but this time, with my sister's permission, I would like to close the show before we have our last few dances."

Pheonna smiled at her sister, nodded and then sat beside me.

"I will need a volunteer for this." Everyone's hands were raised high. The prince even stood up. Pheonna looked at him and smiled. "Not this time, Your Highness. This time I would like Lady Murranda to help me with the trick."

Everyone squealed with enthusiasm and started calling out my name. I was so embarrassed. Phoebe nudged me to get up. Against my better judgment, I got up and walked to the center of the dance floor where Pheonna was standing. I wondered what she had in store for me now.

I also thought about my father and wondered what he was thinking about all this, as he and Jeffery watched from home, through the Murry Rose.

# Chapter 18

I stood in the center of the dance floor next to Pheonna, after she called me to assist her with some magic. I could feel everyone's eyes glued on me. I felt so uneasy and shy I didn't quite know what to do. Then Pheonna walked in front of me and put her hands on my shoulders.

"Let's give Lady Murranda a hand for helping me on this last trick."

After the applause faded, she stared into my eyes. I felt a chill come over me. She waved her hands in the air and a burst of purple fog started to surround Pheonna and me. As the purple fog engulfed the two of us all I could see was the fog and Pheonna.

"Do you think you can take my place with the prince and rule by his side?" she whispered in a frightfully sinister tone.

"I don't know what you are talking about," I responded. "Just because he escorted me to the Ball does not mean Demitri and I are together."

"Demitri you say? You don't even call him Prince. What makes you so special that you can call him by his first name and not by his title? Just because you are some foretold Prophesy? Well, once my plans are fully carried out, the prince will not need any kind of foolish Prophesy to take over all of Xeenoephillia."

"Your plans? What plans?" I dared ask.

"Yes, my plans, and it all starts off by first getting rid of you!" she said, as she scraped my chin with her long nail.

I was about to run off until she pointed at my feet and somehow I could not move them. They were stuck or frozen.

"Now, now, you are not trying to leave before we finish my magic trick for our audience are you, Murranda dear? That would be very rude."

"You are not going to get away with this. I'm sure the necklace your sister gave me has already shown that... that..." I started to explain, until I remembered the real stone of the necklace that showed when I was in any danger was in my room, in the drawer by my bed.

"You were saying, dear," she said with a smirk.

"Well, I'm sure everyone out there must be wondering why this so called trick is taking so long," I said.

"Ha, ha, ha," she laughed. "My dear sweet girl, as of right now, time has stopped outside this fog. Here take a peek," she said. She opened a tiny hole in the fog to show me how very slowly everyone was moving, so slowly it almost looked as if they were not moving at all. Then she quickly closed the hole.

"Well that may be so, but my friends and your prince will soon realize something has happened to me, if I never show up after this celebration is over."

She said, "Oh my, what will I do about that?" She took both her hands and rubbed them across her face and down the back of her hair. When she did that, she somehow transformed into a replica of me. I could not believe what I was seeing. It was like looking into a mirror.

"Mmm, something tells me no one will realize you are missing," she said with my voice coming out of her mouth.

Then she shook her head and transformed back to herself. I was about to scream until she placed her finger on my lips and suddenly my voice was gone. Then, with her same finger, she touched the center of my forehead, and I fainted. Before I hit the floor, I somehow went through the floor.

It was then the pirate Pheonna was working with suddenly grabbed me, put me in a thick sack, and flung me over his shoulder.

"Arrgh, don't take this wrong, me Lady, I personally have nothing against ye. But, if I am going to get me hands on me precious golden weapons my Lady sorceress promised me and me crew, I have to do as she commands. I will try to make it as painless as possible," the captain said as he ran down the castle hall, out of the castle, and headed toward his ship, the Crackon.

After the Captain took Murranda, Pheonna collected herself, and with a single breath, blew the purple fog away to reveal to everyone that Murranda had disappeared.

Once the fog lifted, time went back to normal. No one outside the fog knew what Pheonna was really up to. All they knew was that once the fog lifted, Murranda was gone. Everyone cheered.

Pheonna shouted, "Tada! Thank you again, everyone, for coming to the Dark Castle to celebrate with my sister and me. Now, let the orchestra play," she continued as she pointed to the royal musicians and singers.

"Pheonna, my dear," Prince Demitri said. "Haven't you forgotten something?"

"Have I?" she gasped, with her hand on her face and looking oh so innocent.

"I think you might want to bring back your assistant. I am sure her friends would like to have her back."

"Oh yes, Murranda. I almost forgot. Now what did I do with her? Before I do get her back, I must say adieu, for I have another engagement to attend." Just then, she raised her hands and the purple fog retuned all around, covering the area so no one could see what was happening. "

"If the prince won't make me his bride," she said as she began to transform herself into Lady Murranda, "then I will just have to become his bride." This time she spoke as Murranda and laughed an evil laugh.

# Chapter 19

The audience waited with anticipation to see if Murranda would return. Once the fog settled, "Murranda" walked out, looking a little embarrassed. Everyone cheered, and when the music started to play, the guests grabbed their dance partners and went out onto the dance floor.

Prince Demitri walked up to Murranda, or whom he thought was Murranda, but was really Pheonna looking like Murranda. As he approached her, Pheonna thought to herself, *"Now the real test begins. Let's see if I can fool my prince into thinking I am his beloved Murranda. The most challenging part will be fooling my sister into thinking I am her friend. Will she see though my mask? I better try to steer clear of her, as best as I can."*

"May I say, I have never seen a lovelier assistant," Demitri said as he came closer to her. She blushed, trying to act the way Murranda would act. He took her hand in his hand, and ever so gently, kissed the back of it. "May I have another dance?"

She nodded her head. "Of course you may."

He placed one hand on the small of her back and pulled her in closely. Her heart was racing. *"So far so good. My plan is working. He truly believes I am Murranda."*

As they danced around the Ballroom, she looked to her right and saw Wordorf Leadfoot, one of the Hobbits, starting to walk toward them. Pheonna wanted to use her powers to send him somewhere else, so she could continue dancing with the prince and try to make him fall for her.

She knew she had to make them think she was Murranda, even if that meant dancing with the petty low-lifes. She thought everyone who did not live in the Shadow Land was a low-life.

She also looked around to make sure everyone was still in the Ballroom and that no one had one of Murranda's roses in their possession. If anyone was indeed looking at the rose, they would see that she was not in the Ballroom but on a pirate ship sailing far away from there. Pheonna was determined no one would stop her sinister plan.

As Wordorf continued walking toward them, Demitri looked at her and said, "I guess it would be pretty unfair of me to keep your dance card full and not let our guests dance with the most beautiful one here."

"Your Majesty, I noticed that you have already danced with this lovely lady and I was h…hoping to have at least one d...dance with m...my new friend," Wordorf said, stumbling over his words.

"Of course you may. Anyway, I promised Phoebe and her sister a dance before the night ends."

Demitri handed Murranda over to the Hobbit. He kissed the back of her hand again and excused himself, saying, "My dear, it has been a pleasure as always, but if you'll excuse me now."

She put her hand on Wordorf's shoulder and he led her around the dance floor. She was so embarrassed but tried not to let it show.

*How can I dance with someone that can barely reach my chest?* She thought to herself. She then spotted King Fredrick in the crowd. Using her thoughts, she got the king's attention, and he walked up to the two of them, just as one song ended and a new one began.

"Murry, my dear, I thought I saw your father earlier. Oh well, I'll just have to see him on my way back to my castle after this celebration comes to an end. While I am here, I was hoping to have a dance with my goddaughter," King Fredrick said.

"Oh, Sire, of course you can. Wordorf, I truly enjoyed our dance together," Pheonna said trying not to show her disgust and her surprise.

She had forgotten all about Murranda's father. The last thing she heard about him was that the real Murranda had somehow sent her father and Jeffery back to their home on the Main Land of Xeenoephillia. If that was the case, her plans may already be in jeopardy. If Sir Rudy is home and watching the magical rose, then he already knows that the pirates have taken his beloved daughter on their ship and have sailed away from Xeenoephillia.

*That blundering Captain Darrell better have that little brat safely on his ship, and they better be sailing far away from here.*

Pheonna needed to find a way to excuse herself from the dance floor so she could determine if her plans to get rid of the real Murranda were working. She had to see if there was a way to manipulate the Murry Rose to show something other than her being on a ship. She had to find a way to connect with the rose so it would show everyone Murry was still in the castle and not really on a ship.

# Chapter 20

Meanwhile, on the mainland of Xeenoephillia, Rudy and Jeffery were unaware that they had ever left home to find Murranda. Rudy walked outside of his house and into the Labyrinth Garden to sit by the Murry Rose. He wanted to see how his beloved daughter was doing. He noticed his butler and friend, Jeffery, was already sitting by the rose.

"So I see I'm not the only one worried about her," Rudy said as he placed his hand on Jeffery's shoulder. "So what's been going on?"

"Well, Sire, it seems she has been having a wonderful time in the castle," Jeffery replied, reassuring Rudy that his daughter was fine. "It looks as if the Masquerade Ball has begun."

"What did you just say?" Rudy asked.

"The Masquerade Ball in the Dark Castle is held every year. It is the last big event before the Weekend of Peace celebration comes to an end.

This is a good thing, Sire. It means Lady Murranda will leave the Shadow Land and continue her journey, unless she has already found whatever it is she is looking for. Then she will be heading back here to you to tell you all about her adventures."

"I'm not worried about her journey," Rudy said as Jeffery gave him that, "Oh, really?" look.

Rudy continued, "Well, okay. I am worried. I mean, my daughter doesn't even know what it is she is looking for. Who does that? But when you just mentioned the Masquerade Ball, I had a déjà vu moment."

Jeffery suggested, "Maybe that is because you and Countess Morinda had both attended the same Ball in the past."

"I know that, Jeffery, but I feel it's something else. I can't quite put my finger on it."

Just then, the Murry Rose showed Murranda walking up to Pheonna and then they were surrounded by smoke. The shadow showed Murranda falling through the floor. She was being captured and put into a sack by a man who looked to be a pirate.

"Jeffery, did you just see what I saw?" Rudy said in a panic.

"Yes, Sire, I did!" Jeffery replied as he studied hard on what was going on with Murranda.

"She needs my help! Go get my carriage as I grab a few things. Then you and I are going to save my daughter!"

As Rudy ran inside the house to get what he needed, he passed the large portrait of his wife. He stopped in his tracks and looked at the portrait.

"Don't worry my love. I am going to rescue our daughter. I bet that blood-sucking prince is somehow behind all of this."

He stared at the birthmark on his wife, the tiny star both she and their daughter had. At that point he realized what really happened.

"Jeffery! Come quickly!" He called out.

"Yes, the men have your carriage ready for you."

Rudy started pacing back and forth and kept repeating, "I cannot believe she did this," over and over again.

"Sire?" Jeffery asked. "Are you alright?"

"Not really, Jeffery, and neither are you."

"What does that mean, Sire?"

"Somehow my daughter knows more about who and what she is than we realized. She did the exact same thing Morinda did to me all those years ago."

"Sire, what are you talking about?"

"Look, old friend, you are not going to remember this, but just hear me out. We were at the castle with my daughter and for some reason she found a way to send us back here with no memory of ever leaving this house. My Morinda did the same thing years ago when I tried to get her away from the prince."

"So what are we waiting for, Sire? We need to get back there now!" Jeffery began grabbing the things they would need.

"Let's go, old friend. If we can get to the Forest of Elves, I know they have a way to get us to the Shadow Land and to the Dark Castle quickly. Let's go!"

So Rudy and Jeffery climbed into their carriage and headed quickly to Elfinnia, the Forest of Elves. They hoped some of their elf friends who were still there and not at the celebration would help them get to the Dark Castle more quickly, to rescue his daughter in time.

# Chapter 21

Father and Jeffery began their way back to the Dark Castle in the Shadow Land, hoping to get there in time to save me. Pheonna had everyone in the Dark Castle fooled into thinking she was me.

I was just beginning to regain consciousness. As I awoke, I felt very disoriented, not knowing where I was. The last thing I remembered was being in the Dark Castle enjoying myself at the Masquerade Ball. Then I was called up on stage during the entertainment to help Phoebe and Pheonna with their magic.

I remembered that Pheonna had surrounded the two of us in some kind of purple fog. I was very upset. I knew she was with me for some reason that had to do with the prince. Then I passed out.

Now, it looked as if I were in some kind of cabin or room. All I could see was a dirty, dark wooden table with maps and a compass and lots of empty bottles of rum.

As I became more aware, I realized my wrists were tied together, my knees were brought up to my chest with my arms around them, and my ankles were also tied together. I tried to get loose. I was able to straighten my legs away from my chest.

I quickly brought my tied hands up to my neck to feel for the necklace Phoebe gave me. I wondered why it had not warned me of what was about to happen. Then I remembered. The stone with the ability to warn me of danger was not the same stone I was wearing. Now I wished I had never switched them. Not knowing where I was or how I got here I was really becoming frightened, but I did not want to show it to anyone who might be watching. I was always taught you can be afraid of something, just never let it show.

I heard voices outside the room. One was saying "I think it's time to check in on our special guest, the Lady Murranda."

I wasn't sure what I should do, but I had to find a way out of this mess I was in. For now, I quickly put my knees back to my chest and my tied hands around my knees and pretended to still be unconscious.

Just then, Captain Darrell Braveheart opened the door and said, "Arrgh, wakey-wakey dearie, ye don't want to sleep all day and miss out on the fun."

He started to walk toward me and as he approached, I pretended I was trying to wake up. I moaned and grunted and started mumbling, wondering where I was.

The captain came in so close I could feel and smell his rum-filled breath on my face. I leaned back a little hoping he would lean forward, and when he did, I quickly straightened my legs and kicked him in his privates.

When he bent over in pain, I grabbed his sword with my tied hands and stood up, pointing the sharp blade at his throat as he slowly stood up in pain.

"Arrgh, I see we have a feisty one on board with us today," he said as he coughed.

"On board? What do you mean on board? Where am I exactly, and how did I get here?" I tried not to sound nervous or frightened.

"Now, now, Dearie, I, nor me crew, is here to harm a purty hair upon that purty head of yours. We are just following orders. We ask no questions, as long as we get our booty, our gold."

"ORDERS? Whose orders?"

"Oh don't tell me you don't know by now, after she played her magic trick on you? For some reason the sorceress does not like you."

"Why would she do this?"

"Arrgh! It is not me place to ask why, ye see, as long as me crew gets me golden swords and weapons and other lovely gems as promised. Now, If ye would give me back me sword, before ye hurts yourself missy."

"Hurt myself, you say!" With my hands still tied, I quickly threw the sword at the door, and with all my might I jumped up and flipped over the captain's head toward the door where the sword was stuck. As I landed in front of the door, I slid the sword between my tied wrists so that I could cut the rope. Then I grabbed the sword off the door and used it to untie my legs.

The captain just stood there in amazement. "I'm impressed. I could use someone with your skills on me crew. You could teach me crew members a thing or two."

"Ship? Crew? Where am I exactly?"

"Arrgh, where is me manners. I am Captain Darrell Braveheart at your service, and ye are on me ship, the legendary Crackon."

"Wait! Did you just say I am on a ship? A pirate ship?" I kept pointing the sword at his chest and asked, "Where are you taking me?"

"Our orders were to capture you and set sail to Dragon Island where we would get our treasure. I promise you Murranda… May I call you that?"

I nodded yes to him and he continued, "Me crew and I mean you no harm. Ye are free to walk around me ship as me guest. But I must warn ye, if ye see any other pirate ships approaching, ye might want to stay below. We pirates tend to try and take

233

over each other's ships and crews to gain more power and status," the captain explained as he pushed the pointed part of the sword away from his chest.

"Well, if you don't mind, Captain, I will just keep your sword for my own protection."

"With sword skills like yours, be me guest," he smirked.

I then opened the door, came out of the captain's room, and onto the ship's deck, forgetting I was still in my costume from the Ball. The crew quickly reminded me of that, whistling and yelling at me, trying to get my attention. Even two drunken dwarfs, Scoutt and Erock, tried to come up to me, grabbing at my legs as if they were dogs in heat and my leg was their next date. I kicked both of them away from me and turned back to the captain.

I heard one of them saying, "Mmmm, feisty. Just like I like my women."

"Your woman? She is mine. You went after the last one we saw at the castle, Brother."

"Trust me, Erock, you can't handle this one."

The Captain looked at me and smiled then pointed at a drawer in his room. "Arrgh, I believe me have something ye be able to wear that might be more sea worthy."

I went back into his room and tried to untie the back of my dress. I was having a lot of trouble, but I really did not want to call out to the captain to help me. I did not trust him or his crew, so I kept trying to do it myself.

Just then a beagle jumped on the nearby bed, grabbed one of the lacy strings and started to pull it and wrestle with it. It began to loosen to the point where the dress fell to the ground and I was standing there in my undergarments.

I petted the sweet dog on the head and scratched it behind her long floppy ears. "Thank you, I don't know what I would have done without your help."

The dog just smiled a doggy smile and panted with her long floppy tongue hanging out from the side of her mouth.

I opened one of the drawers and saw a pirate's outfit, so I put it on. It was a little loose for my taste but still better then walking around the ship in a Ball gown. I pulled back my hair and tied it up. Then I noticed some belts and boots beside the dresser. One of the belts had a sword scabbard, so I put that on and found some boots that almost fit. After I finished dressing, I looked at a mirror on the wall. I almost didn't recognize myself staring back at me. Now that I was dressed a little better I headed back on deck to see exactly where we were. I walked up to the front of the ship. All I could see for miles and miles was the ocean's water.

I yelled out to the captain, "Just how much further until we reach this Dragon Island?"

"Oh at least two or maybe three days, Missy," he yelled back from the wheel.

*Great, just great,* I said to myself as I wondered how in the world I would get back to my friends at the Dark Castle. I started to fear I would never see them again. And, I would never see Demitri again, just as I was getting to know more about my mother, more about him and about myself. As upset and worried as I was becoming, I did not let it show to the captain or his crew.

As I looked out upon the open sea, I saw dolphins swimming alongside the ship and seagulls flying overhead. I even saw pelicans flying and swooping down to catch fresh fish.

From a distance I noticed another pirate ship. I turned around and saw the crew all busy doing different things. Some were mopping the deck, others were fixing cannons, while others were climbing up masts to the look-out point, to see what they could see.

I also saw some pirates were fishing on the side of the ship, while others huddled in a group playing cards and drinking. All of them seemed to be enjoying what they were doing. I could hear them humming and whistling and singing pirate songs. It was quite a site.

I looked back out to the sea and noticed the pirate ship I had seen at a distance earlier seemed to be getting closer our way.

I yelled at the captain again, "Captain, oh Captain, I think there is something you and your men might want to see."

"Arrgh, what might that be, Missy, a purty dolphin swimming beside us?" He replied sarcastically acting so male and superior around his crew. His crew laughed.

"No!" I replied, rolling my eyes in frustration, "but a pretty pirate ship is heading our way and they don't look too friendly."

"Oh HELL! " He yelled. "It is that menacing young pirate and his crew led by one of my enemies, Captain Seahan."

"I was wondering when I would see him again. He thinks he can take over my ship. Well, I'll show him who runs these Seven Seas. All hands on deck! All hands on deck! Everyone to your post! Get ready to fire on my command!" He yelled to his crewmen.

"Missy, you might want to go back to the captain's quarters," yelled Scout and Erock, the two dwarf pirates. They tried to guide me back to the captain's room. "It will be safer for you there. We will stay close by your side," Scout said as he tried to grab my butt.

I quickly pulled out my sword and stared at the two of them. "I think I will be fine just where I am," I replied. "

Suit yourself," replied Erock. "See brother, she is not the woman for you, either."

As disgusted as I was with their behavior, I could not help but laugh at the way they behaved with each other. Watching them slapping one another over the head...

I could not believe all that had happened to me. Not only was I captured and taken to a pirate ship to be sailed away to Dragon Island, now I was about to be in the middle of a pirate war. But even with all that going on, I still could not help but wonder what was happening back in the Dark Castle.

Was Pheonna truly fooling everyone into thinking that she was me? What was going on back there?

# Chapter 22

Captain Braveheart and his crew were getting ready to battle the ship that was sailing toward us. Commanding the wheel on that ship stood a young, handsomely -rugged captain. He was tall, well-built and quite well-groomed for a pirate. He had long black wavy hair, a well-groomed goatee and even though his clothes were dirty, they were not torn and ratty looking. He was well spoken and well educated, but in front of his crew he would try to act and sound like most pirates.

Captain Brock Seahan had a deep secret he kept hidden from everyone. If this secret were to come out, he feared there would be a mutiny on his ship. The captain was really a prince, the son of King Fredrick and Queen Katherine of Xeenoephillia.

Brock had become bored with his life as a prince. He craved adventure and excitement. For years he dreamed of a life as a pirate, ruling over the seven seas and becoming the most feared pirate known. He wanted his name to go down in history, just like the legendary Captain Blackbeard.

His parents tried and tried to persuade him to stop thinking about life as a pirate. His father would tell him, "No son of mine is going to take up any kind of life as a pirate."

So Brock told his father he would renounce his title as prince and give up his crown if it meant he could become what he truly wanted to be. His father reacted and told him if he did that he would no longer be his son. He said he would find a way to make their people think Brock was dead.

The prince made his choice, and his life as a pirate began. But he knew that if anyone learned his true identity, his life would be in danger.

Pirates don't live by kingdom laws. They live by their own laws and ways. For that reason, in front of his crew or other pirates, he acted as vicious as they came. He would try to take over any pirate's ship he came into battle with, especially when it came to Captain Braveheart. Most who knew the

Crackon's captain called him "Captain Heartless." Captain Seahan believed if he could get control of the Crackon, it would put him one step closer to possibly being the second-most feared pirate next to Blackbeard himself.

"So, Captain," a crew member yelled out, "the Crackon is just ahead of us. What is your command?"

"Slow and easy, fellas, I have a special surprise for them. Start the fog!" He yelled to the crew below, and they started to blow out the fog so it would cover his ship, which he proudly named the Flying Merlain.

Seahan went down to his cabin and then into a secret compartment below, where he stored his secret weapon. It was a big, bright, blue crystal that laid on top of three darker blue crystals. When he closed the door to his secret room, he turned to the crystals, "Okay my dear friend, it's time to see if you can still do your magic."

He took a vile that was in his vest pocket and sprinkled some stardust on top of the crystals.

Just then, the bright, blue crystal started to float high above the darker crystals, then began to spin. As it spun faster and faster, the captain's ship started to fly.

Across the way, Captain Braveheart was stunned by what he was seeing. The fog appeared out of nowhere and engulfed the Merlain. All he could do was stare in amazement at the fog, as it got closer and closer to his ship and crew, until it covered his ship as well.

Suddenly, the fog began to clear and when it did, Captain Braveheart looked around for Seahan and his ship, not knowing where in the world they could have vanished. One of his men tapped him on the shoulder and pointed up. Darrell looked up and to his amazement; the Flying Merlain was hovering above him.

"How in the....? When in the...? This is bloody witchcraft."

"Witchcraft you say," Brock responded. "Oh no! Let me just say, me old friend, someone I knew gave me a little gift that allows me to do just this and so much more."

Captain Seahan and his crew threw over the ropes and came down from their ship onto the Crackon, and the battle between the pirates began. Punches were thrown and swords were swung with sweat and blood flying everywhere.

Even I had to join in on the fight because Captain Seahan's crew did not know, nor did they care, that I was not part of the Crackon's crew. As far as they were concerned, if you were on a ship, you were fair game.

I prayed I would somehow get through all this fighting and find my way back to Xeenoephillia, back to the Shadow Land and back to the Dark Castle and my friends, and also to Prince Demitri. I had to let him know what Pheonna had done, and was still doing.

I kept fighting for myself and thinking about how I could get back to the ones I loved. I was not paying attention to what I was doing, not realizing I was backing myself onto the ships plank while fighting off some stinking pirate.

One of the pirates cut a rope that held back a beam. Once he cut it, the beam swung around and hit me across the back of my head. It knocked me out and I fell over the railing of the ship, out into the middle of the ocean.

While I was fighting with one of the pirates, my foot became tangled in a rope that was tied to something heavy. When I fell off the ship, the heavy object dragged me down deep into the bottom of the sea.

After I fell overboard the two dwarf pirates, Scoutt and Erock, looked over the railing "Well, there goes another one." Erock said with his lip poking out. "Bye, my-almost-wifie."

"Your wifie?" Scoutt yelled "That was my wifie."

"You think everything is yours." Erock shoved his brother.

"Maybe I do and maybe I don't. And maybe I will take this bottle of rum as a consolation prize."

Scoutt grinned as he hit his brother over the head then took his bottle of rum. And so the brothers kept fighting over me and the bottle of rum.

Captain Braveheart's crew and Captain Seahan's crew continued to battle it out at sea, far away from Xenoephillia, heading towards Dragon Island, with me sinking to my death.

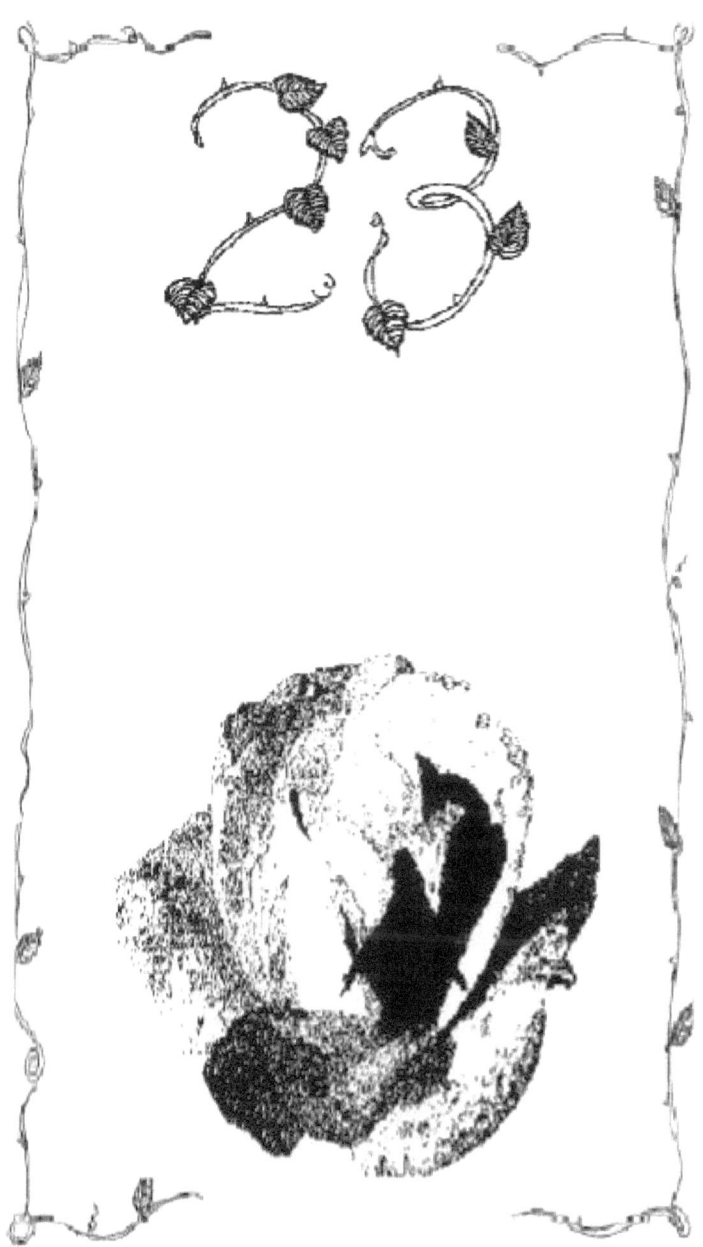

# Chapter 23

Meanwhile, back in the Dark Castle in the Shadow Land in Xenoephillia, the dark sorceress, Pheonna was still working her magic, fooling everyone into thinking she was me. She danced and laughed with all the guests, cozying up to the prince. She had everyone fooled, or so she thought.

Her sister, Phoebe, was standing with Nessa, Jett, Phoenix, Sky, Glitz and Flutter. She kept looking at Pheonna with suspicion. Deena was also feeling unsure of this "Murranda."

Deena walked up to Phoebe and said, "Please tell me I am not the only one who thinks there has been something different about Murry since you and your sister's act ended."

Deena and Phoebe both kept an eye on her. "Speaking of your sister, where is she? It seems after she made Murry disappear and then reappear, your sister vanished herself. As often as I have been coming to these festivals, Pheonna has always stayed till the very end."

"You're right, old friend, my sister wouldn't dare leave the prince's side this long. In fact, lets see if I can find my dear sister," Phoebe said as she took a small feather off her mask, placed it in the center of her left hand and with her right hand she made small circles above the feather.

She then whispered to it, "Little feather in my hand, find my sister if you can." She then blew the feather ever so gently. The feather floated around the room and with a surprising twist, landed on the person they all thought was Murranda. She was once again dancing with the prince. As the feather landed, she tried to brush it off, but the feather kept landing back on her shoulder.

Demitri looked at the feather, then back at her, and smiled, "It seems that feather wants to dance with you as well."

Pheonna looked at the feather on her shoulder. She then looked around for her sister, realizing what was really gong on. She saw her sister walking towards them and asked, "Demitri, can we go somewhere where we can be alone to talk?"

"Of course, but we must wait. The Ball is about to come to an end, and I will have to give my speech and present the King and Queen with a gift. After that, when everyone retires to their rooms, we can have our time alone."

"But I really need to talk to you now," she pleaded as she tried to pull him away from the dance floor.

Just then Phoebe and Deena walked up to the two of them. "Going somewhere Murranda?" Phoebe asked.

"Well, as a matter of fact, the prince and I were just about to leave and go somewhere more private to talk," she said as she tried to take the prince by the hand.

He pulled away from her. "As I told you, I can't just now. You know how it is. You have been to these so many times in the past, Pheonna dear. You know the routine."

She looked at him in shock then quickly laughed.

"Ha, ha, ha, Pheonna? Don't you mean Murranda, silly."

"No! I mean Pheonna!" Demitri replied sternly with disappointment.

Pheonna stepped back and crossed her arms. "So how did you find out? When did you know?"

"I didn't know until I saw how the feather would not leave your shoulder. At that point I knew that feather came from your sister, Phoebe, because it was the same trick my mother taught her when you two were just children and hiding from each other around the castle."

Prince Demitri went on, "When I saw her walk up to us, and the feather finally fell off, it just confirmed what I thought. So tell me, Pheonna, why have you changed yourself to look like Murranda?"

"Yes tell us!" Deena said as she walked right up to Pheonna. "And what have you done with the real Murranda? Tell us now!"

Just then, in a flash, Pheonna turned herself back to the dark sorceress. Then all the guests in the Ballroom stopped in their tracks. Even the musicians stopped playing. The room was in such shock you could hear a pin drop.

When Pheonna took her true form, she held on to the prince's hand. "Sire, you don't need her. You don't need to follow the Prophesy to carry out your plan. With me at your side, I know we can find a way to make it all happen, and you and I can rule all of Xeenoephillia."

Demitri snatched his hand away from her. "How many times do I have to keep telling you Pheonna? I will never see you in the way you want me to. You and your sister are like daughters to me. Now tell me what you have done with Murranda."

Phoebe began to be very concerned about the way her sister was acting. She thought of Murranda's father and realized he was back at his house, looking at the Murry Rose, so if anyone could tell them what was happening to Murranda, he could.

So Phoebe quickly stepped away from everyone and stood by a nearby wall. She sketched an outline of Rudy and Jeffery. Then she stuck her hands through the two sketches and pulled out Rudy and Jeffery. The two men looked around in shock. They shook their heads not knowing what had just happened.

"What…? How….? How did we get here?" Jeffery said scratching his head.

"We were in our carriage and holding the rose and heading here, but we were not even close to arriving," said Rudy in confusion.

"Don't worry, my friends," Phoebe said. "I'll make sure all your things and carriage are returned to you, and I'll explain later how you got here. For now, just be glad you are here. We have bigger problems. Has the Murry Rose shown you what has happened to your daughter?"

"Yes, if we had the rose, we would show you."

Jeffery began looking around for the rose.

Deena heard what Rudy and Jeffery were saying, so without anyone seeing her she bent her head, pointed her horn to the ground and closed her eyes tightly. Just then Rudy's Rose appeared behind him.

"Yes, the Rose. How did it… I thought it was still in the…"

"That doesn't matter now. Look! She is on some kind of ship and sailing away somewhere," he said holding up the Rose so everyone could see. "It also looks as if she is in trouble. There is a fight going on."

He handed the rose to Jeffery when he saw Demitri coming towards him to get a look at the Rose.

"You did this! You blood-sucking son of a…."

"Rudy, wait! Calm down!" Deanna yelled, jumping between Rudy and the prince. "He did not do this. I swear to you."

"Then who did?"

"My sister," Phoebe said with disappointment and anger in her voice, and looking right into her sister's eyes as Pheonna began stepping away.

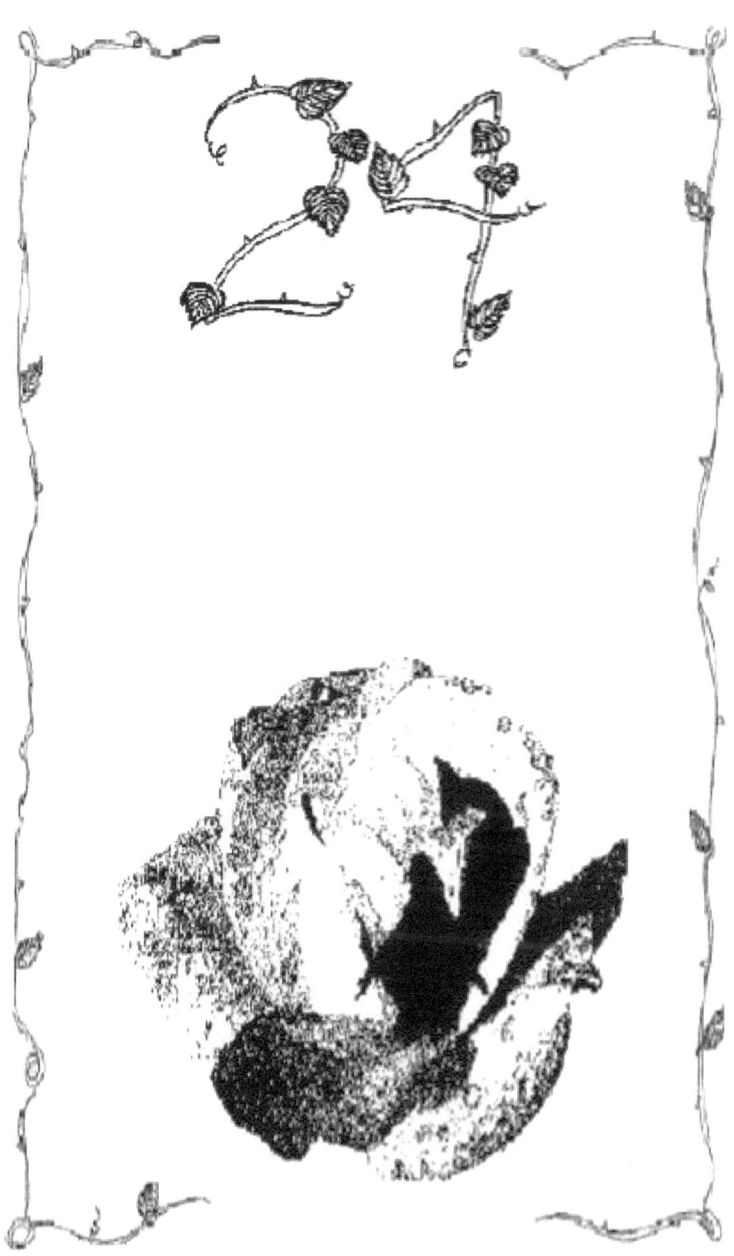

# Chapter 24

Pheonna realized her plan to take over Murranda's life had come to an end. Everyone in the castle was ganging up on her because of all she had done. So she stepped back, raised her arms and waved her hands in the air.

Instantly everyone who owned a magical Murry Rose had it in their hands she then lowered one hand, and poof, she too had one of the Murry Roses.

The white rose was showing everyone that Murranda was on a pirate ship, fighting for her life. Then it let them see when she fell off the plank. They all noticed the wooden beam swinging around and knocking her overboard, causing her to sink into the deep blue sea.

At that point, Pheonna, with her long dark nail, touched the shadow on the rose. When she did, the shadow suddenly got wider and wider, not only on her Rose but on all the roses. The shadow kept getting wider and darker, until it engulfed the entire rose and turned it black as night.

The last thing anyone saw of Murranda was her hitting the cold ocean's water surface and sinking deep into the sea.

Was this the end of their beloved Murry? Everyone stood as though paralyzed in fear, fear for their friend, with tears in their eyes. Even Prince Demitri himself stood staring at the now-black rose, with a blood tear falling down his cheek. Everyone was in tears, except Pheonna. You could hear her cold-hearted cackling laugh throughout the castle.

What was supposed to be the conclusion of a Weekend of Peace celebration ended in a wave of despair, sorrow and wrenching sadness and death? Could this truly be the end of dear Murranda's journey?

# The Murry Rose

# BATTLE FOR THE ROSE
### THE MURRY ROSE SAGA

## C. H. FORTENBERRY

# PREVIEW

Everyone in the Dark Castle stood in the Grand Ballroom and was filled with sadness and disbelief at what the Murry Rose had last shown. Their beloved Murranda had fallen off a pirate ship. (They didn't even know what she was doing there in the first place.) They saw her falling to her death into the cold, shark-infested ocean. Everyone in the castle, including her father, Rudy and the dark Prince Demitri kept saying to themselves, "I can't believe she is gone."

Everyone, that is except Grey Sky, the Camilla cat. Something inside him knew Murranda was not dead. He could not explain it, but he just knew.

He even ran up to Rudy and nudged him on his leg, "Rudy, please don't cry. Murry is okay. She is not dead. I know it. I just know it."

"How can you say that Sky?" Rudy said as he tried to get him to stop nudging. "I don't know how, I just know. She is not dead."

263

Sky tried to calm Glitz, Flutter, Nessa and the rest of the friends. Sky even walked up to Phoebe who was about to take her sister into another room. "Phoebe you have to believe me. I can't explain how, but I just know Murranda is alive."

Just then the prince yelled out, "Guards, take Pheonna away!"

"Sire, wait!" Phoebe yelled. May I follow the guards? I may have a way to help them detain my devious sister."

"Whatever you do to her, make sure she suffers for what she has done to my Sunshine," Rudy cried out as he held tightly to his rose.

Sky kept trying to get someone to hear what he was trying to convey. Just then a tall, slender catlike woman with tiger markings joined them. This was the same being he was in competition with earlier.

"You still don't understand why you are having those feelings do you? If you feel that your Murranda is alive, then she is. The two of you are

264

connected as one. You see, my friend, you are her Guardian."


**Well, my readers, Part III of <u>The Murry Rose</u> will hold answers to many questions: What is Sky's new role in the story? What has really happened to Murranda? What will happen to Pheonna? What about the Prophesy now? Will The Murry Rose ever return back to its natural state? Find these answers and so, so, much more in my next book: THE MURRY ROSE "BATTLE FOR THE ROSE" BY C.H. FORTENBERRY.**

## ABOUT THE AUTHOR

C.H. Fortenberry delivers another installment from "The Murry Rose Saga" Book # 2 of her 6 book series, "The Forbidden Rose." She has been busy growing her brand and also her depth in fantasy writing, public speaking, and promoting her life long dream of becoming a Best Selling Author, Movie Star and house hold name. Her first book "The Murry Rose" found national acclaim as she along with her publishing team ventured out into the world: she headlined a career day at one of Washington D.C's premier Tech Schools, travelled to both ComicCon and DragonCon events, and made big waves at New York City's BookCon 2015. Personal mildstones achieved this year has really become a motivation that has sparked new life into Mrs. Fortenberry, she not only writes but her creative mind has brought all of her characters to life in physical merchandising, action figures, cards, T-shirts and toy concepts. Look for "The Murry Rose Saga!" Taking over bookstores and the big screen this year!